"I know you, Kate Hardie."

Aidan Crawford lifted his hand and caught hold of her chin. "Kate—the eternal virgin, reeling men in with the promise of your sensuality. And when they bore you, you drop them, don't you, Kate? No man could love you more than you love yourself."

Horrified by the picture he painted, Kate couldn't unlock her gaze from his. "That's horrible," she gasped, her heart beating achingly fast.

"The truth often is," he agreed chillingly. "But be warned, Kate. I'm not like any man you've met before. I don't ask or plead, or grovel. I don't play by your rules, only my own." His voice dropped to a husky growl. "I take what I want. Like this...."

Before she could do more than register the shock of his intent, his head had swooped and his lips claimed hers.

D1322550

AMANDA BROWNING is a British author who lives in Essex. She is single and a former librarian. Her lively contemporary writing style appeals to readers everywhere.

Books by Amanda Browning

HARLEQUIN PRESENTS
1055—PERFECT STRANGERS
1329—WEB OF DECEIT
1400—SOMETHING FROM THE HEART

HARLEQUIN ROMANCE
3031—THE ASKING PRICE

AMANDA BROWNING

a promise to repay

Harlequin Books

TORONTO • NEW YORK • LONDON
AMSTERDAM • PARIS • SYDNEY • HAMBURG
STOCKHOLM • ATHENS • TOKYO • MILAN

Harlequin Presents first edition February 1992
ISBN 0-373-11432-X

Original hardcover edition published in 1991
by Mills & Boon Limited

A PROMISE TO REPAY

CHAPTER ONE

IT WAS almost time. Kate Hardie felt her heart start to thud as the adrenalin pumped through her. She glanced down at her hands. They were trembling, but not from fear. For four years she had waited for just such a moment as this, knowing that if she was patient it must surely come. And it had. Yet it had been by sheer chance that she had seen the notice of the engagement in the paper a month ago. To cap it, luck had been on her side too, because it had been quite ridiculously easy to discover the time and place of the wedding. A word in the right ear, and she had known that Aidan Crawford was marrying the Honourable Julia Howell today at three o'clock.

Kate balled her hands into fists. This was her right. An eye for an eye. She owed it to her brother. The memory brought a glitter to her eyes and a tightness to her lips. No man could do what had been done to those she loved and get away with it!

She closed her mind to the sound of cars arriving, of doors opening and closing, and laughing greetings, and didn't try to hold back the memories. It seemed only right that today of all days she should remember exactly why she was here.

She had been twenty-two then, and Philip, her brother, only fourteen. There had been just the two of them since their parents had been killed in a motorway pile-up two years before. Life had not been easy, but they had managed. They had lived in a small flat that her job in an estate agents just allowed her to afford. There hadn't been much money left over for luxuries, but it hadn't mattered because they were together.

Then Philip had become ill. One day he had seemed the happiest, most healthy teenager she knew, and the next he had started to fade away before her eyes. It had felt as if they had visited every hospital, seen every specialist in the country before they finally reached a diagnosis. It was a little-known disease, but a treatment had been found that gave a good chance of recovery. The only problem was that Philip would have to go to America, and the cost of the treatment itself was prohibitive.

She had tried to raise the money, of course, but she had had nothing to sell, and no collateral for the size of loan she required. As her options slowly ran out, so her brother's deterioration seemed to increase its pace. Though she had tried not to show her concern, especially in the face of his stoical cheerfulness, she had been almost frantic with worry by the time she'd remembered Aidan Crawford.

It had seemed like the answer to all her prayers. Her father had once told her—perhaps with some premonition of his early death—that if anything should happen to him and her mother she could go to this man for help. They had been friends for many years and still corresponded. If she had trouble, he would do all he could to help.

And so, filled with a new hope, she had found a London address in the telephone directory and gone to see him.

With a shiver, Kate came back to the present. She glanced outside and saw that the bride had arrived. Soon she would have her revenge for that night, four years ago, when her world had been ripped apart. Philip had been so sick that she had hated to leave him, but there had been no time to waste. So she had gone, and while she had pleaded her cause her brother had been rushed into hospital. Still, there might have been time, if the money had come, to save him, but Aidan Crawford had refused.

She had gone home in an agony of despair, to discover what had happened to Philip, but before she could leave for the hospital she had received a telephone call telling her her brother had gone into a coma. He had died in the small hours of the next day. The double blow had been too much. She had gone into shock, recalling very little of that night beyond Aidan Crawford's refusal which had, to her mind, set the seal on her brother's fate. It had left her with a burning hatred of the man who could have saved Philip, and she had vowed that one day he would pay.

She had remained in shock for days. Not even the sad little funeral had penetrated the ice that had settled inside her. Something vital within her had died. She hadn't been able to feel anything any more, and she hadn't wanted to. Back in the echoing emptiness of her flat, she had known only one thing: that lack of money had given one man the power of life and death over her brother. Wealth could have kept Philip alive, and wealth meant power. A determination was born in her then that, some day, somehow, that wealth and power would be hers.

Barely a week later she had run into an old friend, Rae Purcell. Over coffee they had rekindled that friendship and Kate had discovered that Rae was now a talent scout for a modelling agency. She had rhapsodised over Kate's looks. Anxiety and lack of appetite had worn her always slim, leggy figure into perfect model lines. Grief had fined her face, showing up the good bones and the haughty remoteness in her eyes.

When Rae had suggested that the agency would love that look of icy hauteur, and that she could make a fortune, Kate had been sceptical, but Rae had been right.

Having gone along with the idea simply because it was easier than arguing, almost overnight, it seemed, she had found herself the new sensation. The agency and the advertisers had loved her. In no time at all she had been commanding the sort of money that made the head spin.

Suddenly, the goal she had set herself had come within her grasp and she reached for it with the single-minded energy of one obsessed. She had worked every available hour of the day, going wherever she was asked, knowing that every job successfully completed was money in the bank. Even when she'd become financially secure, she hadn't stopped. Work filled her life. Men were something that made forays into the periphery, but never came close. She worked with them, dined and dated them, but never did they break into her 'real' life.

Besides, she felt nothing. Their kisses and caresses left her cold and unresponsive. Naturally her aloofness, far from being off-putting, was like a red rag to a bull. Someone coined the nickname 'Ice Queen', and it stuck, but she didn't care. Nothing was allowed to interfere with her goal. If a man became too possessive, too intrusive, she dropped him, and that was the end of it.

If it made her enemies, she didn't care about that either. Men had no place in her scheme of things. She was fully aware that each wanted to be the one to 'thaw' her, but only she knew the impossibility of it. So she watched their antics from her lofty position, not amused, but simply indifferent.

But she had never forgotten the vow she had made. With the patience of a cat she had waited—until at last the waiting was over.

Another glance through the tinted rear window of the car revealed a now empty churchyard. The bride and her father had passed inside. Faintly, the opening chords of the bridal march reached her. It was time to go.

Automatically she checked her appearance in the mirror set in the side panel. Reflected back was a face whose beauty fully deserved the epithet 'Ice Queen' that had been bestowed on her. Though she had never met her, Kate had inherited her Nordic blonde looks from her maternal grandmother as well as her name. In repose, hers was a cool and haughty beauty that stated clearly 'look but don't touch'. Yet determination glittered in her cool blue eyes in contrast to the fullness of her lips, which hinted at a sensuality as yet unrealised.

All Kate saw was a control which satisfied her that all was well. Her nimble fingers lowered the veiling of the elegant hat perched atop her head and which hid her long silver-blonde hair. The cerulean blue exactly matched the suit she wore and the high-heeled shoes on her feet. As she edged to the door, she paused to press the intercom button. On the other side of the partition, a uniformed chauffeur lifted his head.

'Turn the car, John, and wait for me here. I shan't be long,' she declared in her cool, slightly husky voice, and climbed out.

Her feet made a satisfyingly determined crunch on the gravel path as she made her way through the lych-gate and up to the entrance. As she had hoped, all eyes were on the four figures grouped before the minister, not on the latecomer. Her own eyes lingered briefly on the tall, dark-haired figure in grey morning dress, but scarcely appreciated the way the material sat upon his broad shoulders and slim hips. For one vital instant her nerves jolted at the sight of him, then in another second she had slipped into the shadows of a back pew on the groom's side, and was opening the hymn book.

It was strange how the mind could work on two separate levels. Her lips formed the words of the hymns and made the necessary responses as the service proceeded, while her thoughts dwelt solely on the moment to come.

They said revenge was a dish best taken cold, and never had she needed to keep a cool head more. When she had made her plans, she had had no doubts that she could do what she intended, and she had none now. Although the flames of hatred burnt inside her as strongly as ever, she knew better than to let the emotion overwhelm her. It had been a long wait, but it was almost over.

'If any man can shew any just cause, why they may not lawfully be joined together, let him now speak, or else hereafter for ever hold his peace,' the minister intoned, and the familiar tension hung on the air as everyone waited, willing the seconds to pass so that they might breathe again.

The silence lengthened. Relief replaced the tension, and it was at that precise instant that Kate's voice rang out clearly around the stone walls and vaulted ceiling. 'I do.'

There was a moment when the silence deepened with shock, and everyone turned towards the rear of the church. Kate rose and stepped into the aisle. With her back to the door, she knew she was little more than a dark shadow against the sunlight. But the congregation were clear to her, and she almost laughed at the varying degrees of stunned stupefaction the faces revealed. Then her gaze fixed on one man.

'He can't marry her. He already has a wife—me,' she declared, and pandemonium broke out.

The noise rose to a crescendo of outrage and disbelief. Then there were people everywhere, blocking out her view of Aidan Crawford's handsome face contorted in fury. Kate used the diversion to walk away. It wasn't part of her plan to wait around to answer questions. Yet in the doorway something compelled her to pause and look back, drawn by a pair of eyes that bored into her. Through a gap she met those grey eyes. For a second it was as if they were the only two people present. Even

the noise seemed to fade. A shiver of pure, unadul-
terated fear ran down her spine, and she stiffened, glad
that he could not see who she was, for she knew she had
just made a very bad enemy.

It took a surprising amount of effort to turn her back
on those mesmerising eyes, but she did, and walked away
on legs that felt strangely weak. Nobody attempted to
stop her retreat, and she went quickly back to her car
and climbed in. She shut the door on an uncomfortable
sensation of having been hounded, telling herself that it
was ridiculous to feel that way after only one look.

'You can take me home now, John,' she ordered, glad
to hear that her voice at least sounded calm, and sank
back against the seat as the car moved smoothly forward.

Closing her eyes, Kate heaved a deep sigh. Finally, it
was over. She had kept faith with herself. She had ruined
Aidan Crawford's life—just as once he had destroyed
hers. Not as devastatingly, perhaps, but it was enough.
She wished him joy of what was left. Let the desolation
that she had lived through be his now.

Deftly, Kate rolled the veiling up from her face. It had
served its purpose. Though her face was well known in
some circles, she doubted if anyone there had recognised
her—especially him. She didn't want him to know. She
wanted him to wonder—and learn to hate her the way
she hated him. Nothing less would do.

For a moment she saw his eyes again—grey spears of
ice, promising retribution. But he was helpless. Her
moment was complete. Revenge, she discovered, had a
sweet taste after all. Reaching forward, Kate opened the
small bar set into the console facing her, and poured
herself a small measure of brandy.

'To you, Aidan Crawford.' She raised her glass in
salute. 'May you continue to burn in hell!' she cursed
him, and with a laugh swallowed the contents at a go.

CHAPTER TWO

LATER that evening Kate stood before the cheval-glass in her dressing-room and smoothed the soft jersey fabric of her dress over her hips. The style was simplicity itself, and something of a trademark of hers. A black shift that clung to every curve, with long tight sleeves and a slit neck that had virtually no shoulders. It emphasised her willowy figure, the skirt ending above the knees of her long, slender legs.

She was dressing for a very special occasion and she was using infinite care, down to the last finishing touches. Her hair she had swept up into a pleat that revealed the swan-like grace of her neck. In her ears, platinum and diamond studs gleamed, and about each wrist she now fastened narrow diamond bracelets. Enough to relieve the plainness of the dress and no more. Make-up she had applied cleverly to give the effect of wearing very little—a technique garnered from her years as a top model, and one she now passed on through the modelling school and agency she had started this year. All in all, she was pleased with what she saw as she slipped her feet into black stilettos.

There was a suppressed gleam in her eyes as she looked forward to the next few hours. Tonight she was crowning her success with a party. A spontaneous idea she had acted on during the drive home, using the car phone to issue her invitations. Down below everything was in readiness. She was about to celebrate the end of a chapter in her life. What had at times seemed an impossible

12

dream had come true. She had bested Aidan Crawford and felt euphoric with triumph.

The distant sound of the doorbell interrupted her silent appraisal, and with a final look she quickly left the room, flicking off the light as she went. Descending the stairs, she heard voices in the drawing-room and her step lightened as she recognised them. Maggie, her housekeeper, turned as she came in, the low-voiced conversation ending abruptly, so that Kate knew she had been the topic under discussion. She frowned. That had been happening all too frequently lately and she wasn't sure she liked it. Yet it was impossible to get angry. Maggie had been with her for four years now, and the older woman had often been part minder, part mother, rather than full-time housekeeper.

Her eyes flickered to the other occupant of the room. The short, dark, slightly plump figure belonged to her friend Rae. Her confidante and, more recently, her assistant. In fact, Rae was the only one who knew what the celebration was about, although Kate sometimes wondered how much Maggie knew and how much she simply guessed about the devil that had driven her young mistress. But the housekeeper could be very close-mouthed when she wanted. Like now, as she took Rae's coat with a significant look before facing Kate.

'I was just telling Miss Purcell that everything's ready. I've left more food in the kitchen and there's plenty of ice in the freezer. Just ring down and let me know if the food starts to run out.'

Kate expelled her breath in an irritated sigh. 'Maggie, you're a dreadful liar. You two are making me paranoid. Just what is it you're conniving behind my back?' She waited a second or two and received no answer. Maggie merely looked solemnly back at her, and Rae's face was expressionless. 'OK, don't tell me, but I promise you this. When I've more time I fully intend to find out exactly what's going on. Meanwhile, thank you, Maggie. It looks as if there's enough here to feed an army,' she declared, eying the groaning table. The housekeeper grinned and went out. Left alone with her friend, Kate turned to find herself being looked at critically. Her brows rose in a haughtily dismissive gesture that had been known to quell strong men. Rae merely ignored it.

'You look like the cat who's got the cream,' she said tartly.

Looking away, a self-satisfied smile curving her lips, Kate adjusted a salt cellar by a thousandth of an inch. 'Do I?'

'So you really went and did it?'

Detecting criticism, Kate turned around. 'I said I would,' she replied shortly. They had had this argument before and she hadn't liked it then. Rae, of all people, should have been on her side.

Which she clearly wasn't as she retorted, 'There's no need to look so pleased with yourself. Think of the poor woman he was going to marry.'

Kate looked away, lips pursed mutinously. 'I have. Though she doesn't know it, I've probably saved her from a lifetime of misery!'

'It pleases you to think so, but two wrongs don't make a right,' Rae pointed out acidly.

'You've always been against it, right from the start!' Kate accused bitterly, feeling uncomfortable and—well, betrayed. 'Why?'

'Because I've seen, first-hand, just what this thirst for power has done to you, Kate,' her friend replied bluntly. 'It's made you a cold, bitter woman. I know what Aidan Crawford did to your brother, but in my opinion it's nothing compared to what you're doing to yourself. You've treated every man as if they were him, turning the screw and enjoying it. You like to see men squirm, don't you? You're proud of it.'

'That's not true!' Kate denied swiftly, hurt by this unexpected attack. How could Rae think that? 'I let them know where they stand. It's not deliberate. What they do then is up to them. Why should I care if they make fools of themselves? Its not my responsibility, for heaven's sake!'

'Isn't it?' Rae queried cynically. 'What about Jonathan?'

Kate stiffened. 'What about him?' she demanded, voice tight and defensive.

'The way you treat him is downright shameful! The man's in love with you!'

'Which is his misfortune, not mine!' Kate shot back.

'Oh, can you hear yourself?' Rae exploded angrily. 'I'd slap you if I thought for one moment it would do any good!'

Genuinely shocked, Kate stared at her. 'If I'm such a terrible person, why do you bother to stay around?'

Rae threw up her hands. 'Because I'm worried about you. This isn't you. I've known you a long time, right from school. You aren't a hard or vindictive woman, Kate, but if you don't change soon then you will be. I know you've been through a lot, but you can't keep treating people the way you do. So far they've all been gentlemen, but one day one of them isn't going to take kindly to the brush-off. You could get badly hurt,' she finished in genuine concern, and Kate lost her own anger as she found herself on more familiar ground.

'You worry too much. I can look after myself,' she reassured her friend, smiling.

'Famous last words,' Rae commented wryly. 'Oh, well, I've done my best. I should remember good advice usually goes ignored.'

Kate laughed and bent down impulsively to kiss her friend's cheek. 'I'm glad you care, but really, there's no need.' The doorbell went again as she straightened.

'There are the others. Remember, this is supposed to be a party. Forget to be disapproving and enjoy yourself. It's what I intend to do.'

And she did, flitting from one laughing group to another, on a high that had little to do with the glass of champagne she held. Revenge had acted on her like a powerful drug and she glowed like a neon sign. Never still, she was everywhere making sure everyone had enough to eat and drink, so that it was almost eleven before Rae caught up with her again when she came to rest at the now much depleted food table.

'I see Jack Lancing's here,' she referred to the TV celebrity who had caused quite a stir when he arrived half an hour ago. 'You know he's a wolf in wolf's clothing, don't you?'

Kate swung round in exasperation. 'Oh, Rae, not again, please! Besides, what's so special about his being here? He attends lots of parties.'

'The grapevine's been linking your names for the past two weeks, that's what's special. The man is trouble with a capital "T".'

Kate topped up her glass of champagne and sipped at it appreciatively before answering. 'So am I. Didn't I prove that today? I know very well what Jack wants, and you know he isn't going to get it. In the meantime, it can't hurt me to be seen with him. We're good publicity for each other.'

Rae snapped her teeth on a harsh comment and took a breath. 'And what about Jonathan? You've ignored him ever since he arrived. Do you think that's fair?'

Kate followed Rae's glance to where a sandy-haired man stood brooding over a drink in a corner. 'I can't stand a man who sulks. Good heavens, he knows almost everyone here! It wouldn't hurt him to mingle!'

'He told me you invited him to dinner, and he turns up to find a party!'

'The invitation was made over a week ago. I hadn't planned the party then,' Kate shrugged, ignoring a tweak of conscience that reminded her that she'd forgotten all about Jonathan, her mind taken up with Aidan Crawford.

'That's no excuse and you know it! You can't use people like this.'

Kate scowled. Why did Rae constantly rehash this old complaint? Tonight she could have done without it. 'I treat people the way they treat me.'

'No, you don't,' Rae contradicted swiftly, 'you treat them the way Aidan Crawford treated you, callously. But you fail to realise that they aren't all like him.'

'I'm not going to give them the chance to be. I don't ask for anything, and I don't give anything!' Kate declared fiercely.

'Honestly, Kate——!' Rae began, but was interrupted by the strident ringing of the doorbell.

Kate was relieved. She hated arguing with her friend. Rae just couldn't accept that she was quite happy with the way she lived her life. 'Saved by the bell!' she quipped, then frowned, for whoever was outside had their finger set firmly on the button. Wondering who on earth it could be, Kate swiftly excused herself and made her way into the dimly lit hall.

The irritating clamour went on and on. 'All right, all right, I'm coming!' she muttered fiercely, flinging the door wide and preparing to give the impatient caller a piece of her mind. In the event, she only managed to utter one word, and that a croak, as she saw exactly who stood on her doorstep. 'You!' she gasped, in mingled shock and horror.

'Celebrating?' Aidan Crawford queried contemptuously, his icy eyes dropping to the glass in her hand, then passing beyond to where the noise of the party spilled out.

At the sound of his voice, Kate rediscovered the ability to move and speak. She lifted her chin. 'As a matter of fact, yes, and you weren't invited,' she informed him coldly and slammed the door closed.

At least, she would have done if he hadn't thrust his foot into the gap to stop her. All her strength was nothing compared to the force that flung the door wide again. Kate was compelled to take a hasty step backwards to avoid injury.

'Oh, no, you don't, you little bitch!' Aidan Crawford snarled as he stepped inside, and she couldn't help but fall back before his determined advance.

Only a step or two, though, before her pride brought her to a halt, her eyes flashing fire. 'How dare you? Get out, before I have you thrown out!'

He closed the door with an ominous thud. 'Thrown out? I don't think so, lady. You and I have some talking to do.'

A red rage seemed to burst before her eyes, and she lifted her hand as she stepped forward, wanting to strike out at that hated face. But the blow never landed. He foiled her easily, catching her wrist in a grip that burnt and choked off the blood, making her wince in pain.

'Kate? Are you all right?' Unnoticed, Rae had come out into the hall, brought by the noise, along with several of the others. Her eyes became saucers when she saw who it was, obviously recognising him from his many appearances in the newspapers. 'Oh, my goodness!'

Before Kate could utter a word, Aidan Crawford was speaking. 'This is a private argument. I'm sure *Kate* doesn't want it made public, do you?' He appealed to her, but his look was a threat.

Even so she might well have ignored it if she hadn't glanced at their audience and seen the gleam of delight at her predicament in more than one pair of male eyes. It told her clearly that a call for help would go unanswered. They were all on Aidan Crawford's side, silently willing him on to deliver the come-uppance they considered was long overdue. Even Rae looked uncertain, and that made Kate lift her chin.

'No,' she concurred stiffly.

His smile was grim, and she knew he hadn't missed the atmosphere. Looking about, he spied the door on the opposite side of the hall. 'We'll go in here.' He opened the door and literally propelled her into the dark room ahead of him. 'Excuse us,' he added in mock politeness before shutting the door pointedly. 'Where's the light?' he demanded as Kate struggled to free herself from his grasp. 'Damn it, keep still, or you'll only get hurt. Now where's the damned switch?'

'Behind you,' Kate gritted through her teeth. A second later she blinked as light flooded the room, revealing a comfortable sitting-room before he adjusted the dimmer to a low glow that threw shadows everywhere. Kate had eyes only for the man who still held her fast, and they glittered with all the loathing that was in her. With his back to the light, his menace was even more pronounced. 'Take your hands off me!'

She was released with an alacrity that would have been insulting if she hadn't been so angry. Kate was trembling with the force of it. She could feel it as she rubbed life back into her wrist. 'Don't ever touch me again.'

This time the flashing eyes were his. 'Why should I ever want to? Believe me, once is enough,' he declared with deliberate offensiveness.

Colour flooded her cheeks, and just as quickly faded again, leaving her white-faced. 'My God!' She turned quickly on her heel and crossed to where the telephone sat on a small table. Her hand came to rest on the receiver. 'If you don't leave my home this instant, I shall call the police.'

Far from being alarmed by the threat, he started across the floor towards her. Or so Kate thought, until, too late, she realised what he was actually doing. With a cry of dismay, she watched helplessly as he bent to the small wall fitment and brutally disconnected the telephone.

'You're calling no one until you've answered some questions, sweetheart.' There was nothing endearing about that endearment, and to punctuate his point he placed himself pointedly between her and the door.

Kate refused to be quelled although her nerves jolted. To have Aidan Crawford here, in her house, was something she had never dreamed of. It had thrown her completely. Rather belatedly she realised how incriminating her reaction must have been, and tried to bluff her way out. 'I'm afraid macho tactics don't impress me, Mr... Perhaps you could start by telling me just who you are and what exactly you mean by barging into my house!'

He looked her up and down, his disgust at the tactic apparent. 'It's a little late in the day to start playing ignorant. You knew who I was the instant you opened the door. You also know why I'm here. So let's quit playing around shall we?' he advised cuttingly, a dangerous edge to his voice.

Kate stared at his grim face for a moment or two before moving over to an armchair. Sitting down, she crossed one shapely leg over the other, and relaxed. Or rather pretended to. There was altogether too much tension in the air for that. It registered in the way her fingers tightened on the plush arms before she made them relax.

Her blue eyes were mockingly defiant as she looked at him. From what he said, he clearly recognised her, but if he imagined she was still the gullible fool he remembered he was in for a rude awakening. 'How did you find me?'

A reluctantly appreciative laugh came from him and he shook his head. 'My God, you're cool! You could be talking about the weather! Is wrecking lives a hobby with you? Does it give you a buzz, playing God?' The anger in him was awesome.

Kate's heart raced, but she had long ago learned the art of hiding her emotions. It was part of her stock-in-trade. 'This time it did, certainly—and you haven't answered my question.'

His teeth came together in an audible snap. 'I, too, have friends. One of them took the number of your car. Another pulled strings to find out who it belonged to.' He closed the distance between them in what Kate could only describe as a menacing prowl. 'Surely you knew I'd have a burning desire to see you? To have a cosy little chat about this and that.'

She certainly wasn't about to tell him she hadn't contemplated the possibility. 'I have absolutely nothing to say to you.'

Aidan Crawford's hands clenched, and he thrust them angrily into the pockets of his trousers. She realised two things then: that he would rather his hands were about her throat, and that he still wore morning dress. A detached part of her mind registered that the clothes suited him, and that he must have lost some weight. Her memory conjured up a more heavily set man. But that didn't stop him being far too tall and overwhelming. His very presence dominated her room as he wanted to dominate her.

'Well, I've got plenty to say to you. Just who the hell are you, Ms K. Hardie, and who gave you the right to do what you did today?'

Who was she? What kind of game was he playing now? Immediately her anger resurged. 'You know damn well who I am! I swore you'd be sorry, and I hope you are!'

Grey eyes narrowed to slits in a face that seemed carved from granite. 'Lady, you're crazy. I've never seen you in my life—before today. But I don't think I'm ever likely to forget you!'

'And that's exactly the sort of answer I'd expect from someone like you!' Giving up all pretence of relaxation, Kate jumped to her feet and paced angrily away. 'You make me sick! It's all a game to you, isn't it—destroying people's lives? Well, today you had a taste of your own medicine, and I hope it chokes you!' she spat out contemptuously.

'Why, you little——' he bit off the rest with an iron control. 'It wasn't just my life, was it? What about Julia?' he demanded coldly.

Kate laughed triumphantly. 'She may not know it, but I did her a favour. At least I saved her from discovering what a swine you are the hard way!'

He stared at her incredulously. 'My God, you're insane!'

'It's no thanks to you that I'm not!'

Once more his eyes narrowed. 'Meaning?' he growled.

Kate crossed her arms. 'Oh, come on, Mr Crawford,' she sneered. 'This is Kate Taylor-Hardie you're talking to.' She saw the flicker of recognition in his eyes and her lips thinned. 'So, you do remember me after all. I thought you might.'

That he was holding on to a violent temper by the merest thread was patently obvious as he spoke in clipped tones. 'I vaguely recall a Christopher Taylor-Hardie, but he died some years ago. Are you telling me you're a relative?'

As if he didn't know! 'All right, if you insist on playing this ridiculous game, I have no option but to go along with it. Christopher was my father.'

'Your father?' It was clear from his tone that she had surprised him. 'I had no idea he had children, but then——'

Kate interrupted him with an angry gasp. This was intolerable! 'That's a lie!'

Grey eyes flashed a warning she couldn't ignore. 'I'm getting sick and tired of being called a liar by you, *Ms* Hardie. My acquaintance with your father was brief. I doubt he ever discussed his children. So how could I possibly know of your existence?' he ground out harshly.

Now, now she had caught him out in a blatant lie! 'How? I'll tell you how! Because four years ago I came to you for help, Aidan Crawford. I'm hardly likely to forget that you turned me down!' Nothing could ever wipe out *that* memory.

Whatever reaction she expected, it wasn't the one she got. Aidan Crawford went absolutely still, then very slowly he took his hands from his pockets. Kate could almost see the cogs turning in his mind, and the wariness that came into the eyes that never left her face.

'You came to *me* for help?' There was a curious quality in the question that she couldn't pinpoint.

'For Philip,' she corrected shortly, watching the play of emotions on his face as he searched for a memory.

'Philip?'

'My brother,' she ground out painfully. 'Before he died, my father told me that if ever we were in trouble we could come to you. And I believed him!' She uttered a harsh bark of laughter. 'More fool I! You could have helped, but you didn't, and Philip died. He was fourteen years old! He may have been desperately ill, but there was the chance of a cure. A chance you refused to give him!'

A change came over him. He was still angry, but for the moment, other emotions had surfaced. Ones whose source she couldn't guess at. 'I see. I had no idea, but I begin to understand. The man your father knew, the one he advised you to contact, was *my* father. I was named for him. Surely the age difference would have told you that?'

Momentarily diverted, Kate frowned. 'My father was a professor; it was quite possible for him to befriend a younger man. He was only forty-two when he died.'

Aidan Crawford nodded. 'That's true, whereas, in fact, my father was older than him. But that doesn't change the facts. At the time of your brother's death, I wasn't even in this country. I never saw you.'

The conviction, the absolute certainty in his tone stunned her for a moment. She wondered if she was indeed going mad. But she knew. Damn it, she knew! 'Oh, how could you say that? I saw you as clearly as I'm seeing you now, on the very day Philip...died,' she challenged angrily.

A nerve began to tick away in his jaw. Kate saw it quite clearly as he came to stand before her, though the subdued lighting threw shadows over half his face.

'You saw me? We were this close?' he asked quietly.

Her stomach lurched. 'Yes, we were this close,' she choked out thickly.

'Then you must have seen this,' he stated softly, and turned his face to the light.

Kate gasped. 'This' was a silvery scar that stretched from the left side of his mouth, over his cheekbone, to the corner of his eye. Her hand flew to her throat. 'How did that happen?' The question issued in a whisper, her eyes reluctantly lifting to lock with his.

'In a cricket match, when I was ten,' he informed her, still in that same soft tone. His lips twisted. 'Someone took exception to being bowled out.'

Her eyes rounded in horror. Not so much at the thought of the vicious attack, but at the other implication. 'No! It's impossible! You can't have...you didn't have a scar!' she cried, head reeling.

'Andrew doesn't have a scar.'

The statement slammed her heart against her chest. 'W-who?'

'Andrew—my twin brother.'

There was something in his eyes which said he was telling the truth, but Kate couldn't believe him. To do so would mean . . . 'You're lying. It's just another trick. I don't believe you!'

Her denial didn't anger him, instead he looked resigned. 'I shouldn't imagine you would.' His hand went inside his coat and drew out a wallet. 'Fortunately I have my passport on me, expecting, as I was, to be using it for my honeymoon.' The observation was dry, but Kate scarcely registered it. She was too caught up in studying the photograph he was showing her. The face was his, complete with scar, and so was the name: Aidan Crawford. Yet it proved nothing, and she said so. He smiled grimly and pulled a photograph from the wallet. 'This was taken some years ago now, but it should prove, beyond doubt, that I'm telling you the truth.'

There were four people in the picture, taken on a sunny day on the lawn of a large house. A family scene of husband and wife, and two sons—identical save for the still recent scar one bore on his left cheek. Kate closed her eyes.

'They never could tell us apart, until he gave me this,' he observed, and she opened her eyes again to see him fingering the silver scar broodingly. He retrieved passport and photo and returned them, with his wallet, to his coat.

Kate felt all the fight drain out of her. She could scarcely take it in, and yet it was all too horribly true. A pain shot through her temple, and she lifted trembling fingers to massage the spot. She had to think! Inevitably her eyes were drawn to where Aidan Crawford stood watching her, face devoid of all expression.

'Are you saying that I . . . that . . . ?'

'Asked Andrew for help, not me,' he confirmed. 'I'm afraid my brother has a warped sense of humour. If he could do me an ill turn, he would. Up to and including pretending to be me.' He supplied the rest in a flat tone that she suspected hid a great deal.

Kate was appalled. 'Oh, God!' she gave a moan of disgust. 'What have I done?'

'Precisely. What have you done, *Ms* Hardie?' The icy sarcasm stung, as it was meant to.

She paled and glanced away, mind dazed by what she had learnt. 'How could I know? I thought he was you. I've hated you with every breath I took,' she confessed in an anguished whisper.

'Because you believed I was the one who refused to help Philip?'

Her head jerked up, she'd almost forgotten he was there. 'Yes, because of Philip. I wanted revenge.'

Aidan Crawford breathed in deeply. 'And so you took it today—against the wrong man.'

Kate knew that, however softened his tone, the anger had not lessened. She gathered together the tatters of her lost composure and drew it on. 'Against the right man, as I thought. I was ignorant of there being two of you.' If she had only known, perhaps...but it was too late for 'if's.

'Do you think that excuses your actions today?'

Of course it didn't, but she had been thrown to the wolves once by a Crawford, and it wasn't going to happen again. She drew herself up proudly. 'I don't ask to be excused. I did what I had to do, and I can't be sorry for that.'

'So you have no remorse about destroying two sets of hopes at a blow?' he demanded with a cutting edge she felt keenly.

'Would your brother have felt remorse?' she challenged back.

'No,' he stated baldly.

'And what of the real Aidan Crawford? Would he have turned Philip down?'

A grim smile curved his lips. 'We'll never know, will we?'

'That's tantamount to saying yes. You Crawfords stick together! Remorse? I'm only sorry it was the wrong man!'

'Somebody has to take responsibility for what happened today, and that somebody is you, *Ms* Hardie. What do you intend to do about it?'

Perhaps she had done wrong, but she would never admit it to this man. Who, by his own admission, was as bad as his brother! Schooling her features, Kate returned to her seat. 'Do? I don't intend to *do* anything. And I certainly don't intend to let you make me feel guilty.'

He looked at her as if she was a species he hadn't encountered before and had only contempt for, now that he had. 'But you are guilty. As guilty as hell, and we both know it. You owe me, Kate Hardie.'

She lifted her chin at the coldness in his eyes. 'I owe you nothing. As far as I'm concerned, the Crawford family deserves all that it gets.'

Aidan Crawford drew himself upright. 'Don't make the mistake of underestimating me, Ms Hardie. You owe me, and that's a debt I intend to collect, with interest.'

He meant it, and at that male threat her stomach knotted despite her will. To combat it, she raised her brows disdainfully. 'You can try, but you won't succeed. It wouldn't be wise for you to underestimate me, either.'

He smiled thinly. 'Oh, I won't. I've seen what you can do, but you're out of your depth. I hope you know how to swim, because you're going to need to.'

Kate rose gracefully, lips curved into the faintest of smiles. 'I'm impervious to threats. I'm not the gullible fool I was four years ago. I've learned a lot since then. I've learned to hate, and that's strengthened me against men like you and your brother. So, if you've said all you had to say, you'd better go. You're interrupting my party.'

Aidan Crawford looked her up and down. 'Vengeful and unrelenting. Remorseless and cold. The perfect Ice Queen, *Ms* Hardie.' He used her nickname contemptuously.

'Precisely,' Kate returned, refusing to rise to the bait. 'So I very much doubt that you'll be collecting your debt,' she finished sweetly.

To her chagrin, he laughed. 'Did you think I referred to payment in kind? Oh, no, Kate, there's nothing about you that would tempt me to risk frostbite. There are other ways of paying a debt, and in your case undoubtedly more pleasurable.'

Just why that taunt should have stung so, she couldn't imagine, but it did, and her cheeks flushed. 'I'm relieved to hear it. And now, Mr Crawford, would you kindly get out of my house?' she snapped.

Having shot a bow at a venture and seen it strike home, Aidan Crawford smiled and walked over to the door. 'I'm going, but I'll be back. You can count on it.' With that parting shot, he left. A few seconds later, Kate heard the front door open and close.

As it did, all the strength seemed to drain from her legs and she had to reach hurriedly for the mantelpiece to keep herself upright. Suddenly she was shaking so violently that her teeth chattered. All the hard-won cool composure fled, as round and round her head went the same words—he was the wrong man.

With a groan she rested her forehead on her hand. Triumph had become disaster. How Andrew Crawford must be laughing! Her conscience, subdued by her need for revenge, rose to smite her. She had sown the seeds of destruction on two innocent people instead of reaping the looked-for harvest. No matter what she had said to Aidan Crawford, the guilt *was* hers. But accepting that didn't mean she would give in to threats! The thought of it stiffened her spine a little. In the wrong she may be, but she didn't believe there was anything he could do to her, threaten all he might. Besides, there was nothing she *could* do now. The milk had been spilt.

Kate raised her head and met her own eyes in the mirror. Rae's words came back to her. Was she really a vengeful and bitter woman? Steeling herself, she took a long, hard, honest look at herself—the person she had become in these last four years. Rae *was* right. She was on a path that would turn her life into a wasteland. Unless she altered course, she'd have to watch as that person in the mirror grew into a sour, embittered, lonely old woman!

The thought was too awful to contemplate, as was the memory of the two lives she had just ruined. It was too late to help them, but was it really too late for herself? Couldn't she prove Rae wrong? Did she want to? The answer was an unequivocal yes. She had been cold-blooded and vindictive because she hadn't cared about anybody or anything. Indifferent to whom she hurt or how. Brutally honest now, she acknowledged sickly that she had walked over people's feelings and enjoyed it. Had enjoyed her power over men particularly. It was a savage indictment but she didn't spare herself. She had been wrong, and she had driven herself at such a pace that she had lost touch with how to be a human being.

She shivered. What if she was too late? But no, it couldn't be, otherwise she wouldn't have been given this chance to change direction. Yet what did she do now? Philip was dead, her victory turned to tragedy. She had more money than she could ever spend, so there was no need to work all the hours God sent. All of a sudden, she felt aimless, a little lost and very much alone.

What on earth did she do with the rest of her life?

The soft tap on the door made Kate jump, so deep in thought had she been. She looked up, disorientated, the party only a vague memory.

'Who is it?' She was glad to hear her voice sounded normal.

'Only me,' Rae announced as she came in. 'I heard him go. When you didn't immediately come out, I thought I'd better come and see if you were all right.' Hazel eyes registered her concern.

Kate sighed deeply, feeling exhausted. 'Surprisingly enough, I'm fine.'

'I can see you are. Personally, I thought you'd come to blows. I've never seen a man so angry.'

Heat scorched her cheeks. 'Yes, well,' Kate muttered diffidently, 'he had a right to be.'

'Had a right…!' Rae exclaimed, then frowned darkly. 'Run that by me again. I could have sworn you said——'

'I did,' Kate interrupted before her friend could get into her stride. 'He was the wrong man, Rae. The Aidan Crawford I knew had no scar, whereas this one, the real one, has had one since he was ten. Given to him by his twin brother, Andrew.'

'Twin brother?' Rae sat down heavily on the couch. 'Then it was Andrew who… Oh, Kate, you'd better tell me everything.'

Sitting beside her, Kate outlined their conversation as briefly as possible, reliving her own shock in the telling. Rae was alternately shocked and angry.

'Of course you couldn't have known,' she said, when Kate fell silent. 'Not only the wrong Aidan, but the wrong twin too! Who would have thought his brother could be like that? The thing is, what *are* you going to do?'

'There's nothing I can do to undo what I did,' Kate replied softly, voice laden with guilt.

'I suppose not,' Rae admitted. 'He can't take you to court, can he? I mean, is there a law about claiming to be someone's wife when you're not?'

Kate pulled a face. 'If there is, I'm sure I'll find out,' she said drily.

'Don't joke, Kate, this is serious!'

'I assure you, I don't find it funny,' Kate confessed as she stood up again. 'Come on, we'd better see what the others are up to. Its very quiet.'

'That's because they've all gone,' Rae explained, following her out. 'Jack Lancing began the exodus. He suddenly remembered somewhere he just had to be. I don't think he wanted to be here if the police were called in. Wouldn't suit his image.'

Kate stopped and looked over her shoulder, one eyebrow raised. 'Naturally I assume you threw yourself bodily in his way to stop him?'

Rae grinned, unrepentant. 'I'll be bruised for weeks to come.'

A reluctant laugh escaped from Kate's lips. 'You're incorrigible! But I'm glad you're my friend. I've a feeling I may be needing you.' She hesitated and then said somewhat diffidently, 'I've decided you're right. It's time I sorted myself out.'

'Oh, Kate! I think I'm going to cry!' Rae declared, moisture flooding her eyes.

Kate shifted a lump in her throat. 'Don't you dare, or you'll start me off!' she ordered huskily. 'I...don't feel very proud of the way I've behaved. If only I'd realised before it was too late,' she murmured remorsefully.

With ready sympathy, Rae reached out to squeeze her arm. 'It was like a fever, Kate. It had to run its course.

Just to hear you speak this way... Well, you don't know how long I've waited to say "welcome back". I'll be here if you need me, all you have to do is ask.'

Choked, Kate wondered how close she had come to losing a friendship she really valued. 'Thanks,' she said gruffly, and it came from the heart. Fighting emotional tears, she pulled a face. 'Oh, well, let's go and survey the damage.'

Much later, she wearily climbed the stairs to her bedroom, feeling much as the Ancient Mariner must have done when he'd shot the albatross. Events were set upon a course she couldn't change no matter what she wished. The real Aidan Crawford had exploded into her life and turned it upside-down. Nothing would ever be the same again.

She didn't know just how prophetic those words were to be.

CHAPTER THREE

SUNDAY mornings were generally the only days of the week that Kate got to lie in, and usually she looked forward to it. This particular Sunday morning, however, she awoke early, her body bathed in perspiration, her mind haunted by the lingering fragments of a nameless fear. She sat up, feeling the fine tremors that still shook her limbs, breaths shallow and heart still racing. She could remember nothing, only echoes of unnamed things that had turned her dreams into a nightmare.

She must have had them before, everyone did at some time or other, but she could never recall feeling quite this degree of terror. Brushing her hair from her eyes, she climbed from the bed and went into her bathroom, drawing a glass of water and drinking it thirstily. Her eyes met their reflection. Why now? Was it her conscience talking or an isolated incident brought on by stress?

Yes, surely that was what it was. To say yesterday had been stressful was putting it mildly. It was stress, so there was no need to get worked up because the remnants lingered in her mind like curling fingers of mist. She could dispel it. Work was the answer, some furious activity that would thrust the residue from her and allow her to relax. Fortunately there was plenty of that.

Showering swiftly, she dressed in jeans and sweater, and went downstairs to tackle the mountain of washing-up she and Rae had stacked in the kitchen the night before. It worked, but only to a degree. For with the nightmare dismissed, although her hands were busy, her brain wasn't, and her mind had a disturbing tendency to wander. Things she had said and done these past four years rose up like ghosts to haunt her. Each new flashback brought a shudder as her resurrected conscience pricked her. It was like seeing a picture of someone intensely familiar, and yet a total stranger. Her behaviour had been so outrageous that it was a wonder Rae's prediction hadn't already come true.

That didn't bear thinking about, and she shook her head, reaching out to switch on the radio, drowning her thoughts in music. She didn't hear Maggie come in half an hour later, and stand silently watching as she vigorously wielded the dishcloth. Consequently she jumped violently when a hand reached by her to switch the radio off.

'Goodness, Maggie, you gave me a scare!' she exclaimed weakly, hanging on to the sink.

'So I see,' Maggie observed, looking her over critically, and not missing one of the signs of her troubled night. 'Something must be bothering you, to get you down here at the crack of dawn washing-up. Especially when there's a perfectly good dishwasher in the corner.'

Kate turned back to the sink and fished around for another glass, uncomfortable with the other woman's perception. 'I thought the activity would help.'

'And did it?'

'Yes and no,' Kate admitted with a sigh. Pausing, she glanced over her shoulder. 'You may as well know, I did something pretty awful yesterday.'

Maggie's brows rose. 'And now you're feeling bad about it?'

Kate nodded. 'That and a lot of other things.'

The older woman rolled her eyes heavenwards. 'The saints be praised! I was beginning to think the day would never come. Here, let me look at you.' Careless of the dripping cloth, she took Kate by the shoulders and brought her face to face. 'Yes, there she is. A little ragged around the edges, maybe, but the Kate I heard so much about.'

Kate's colour fluctuated and a lump rose in her throat. 'Not you, too, Maggie?' she protested in a croak. 'You've been talking to Rae.'

'Didn't need to. I've got eyes in my head. All she did say was to look after you, because you were hurting. Don't blame her. She loves you and she's been worried about you,' Maggie declared, releasing her with a suspicion of moisture in her eyes. 'She said you never cried for your brother, and I could see there was such an anger in you. But it's gone. Whatever happened yesterday, it's gone, and I for one am not sorry.'

Kate felt humbled. Now she realised what all those hastily broken-off conversations were about. There had been so much she had been unaware of. 'Neither am I, Maggie, neither am I,' she confessed, and they exchanged a smile of understanding.

Clearing her throat, Maggie reverted to her usual briskness. 'Ah well, this won't buy the baby a bonnet! I'll get started on the lounge and leave you to it.' Collecting the dustpan, brush and duster from a cupboard, she went out again.

Leaving Kate a prey to more thoughts she found uncomfortable. From the reaction of the two people closest to her, her behaviour had been pretty obnoxious since Philip died, but it was a measure of true friendship that they hadn't given up on her. She probably deserved that they had, but she was inordinately grateful that they hadn't.

With another shake of her head, she returned to the dishes, washing and drying them, and had just begun to stack them away when Maggie reappeared.

'Must have been a wild party,' she observed, checking the water in the kettle before switching it on and reaching for the teapot. 'Somebody ripped out the telephone in the sitting-room.'

For the second time that morning Kate jumped, colour darkening her cheeks. She wondered how on earth she could have forgotten the incident—but then, so many things had happened last night. As the unwelcome reminder of Aidan Crawford recalled. She was glad she had a legitimate reason to turn her back as she stacked plates in the cupboard. 'Oh, yes, the telephone. Um...things did get a little out of hand for a while.' What an understatement that was!

Maggie paused in the act of spooning tea into the pot. 'You should have rung down. John would have come up to help.' Her husband was Kate's chauffeur-cum-gardener, and they lived in a cottage in the grounds of Kate's house.

'Oh, it wasn't that bad,' Kate reassured hurriedly. 'I soon sorted it out.' She crossed her fingers to negate the blatant lie. 'You'd better arrange for someone to come and repair it tomorrow.'

The tea made, Maggie carried two steaming mugs to the table and sat down. 'John will fix it. More to the point, you'd better make sure you don't invite that particular party here again.'

That made Kate laugh with genuine humour as she joined the other woman. 'It's OK, Maggie. I've no intention of doing so.' However, the amusement faded as she drank her tea. Not inviting Aidan Crawford was one thing to decide and another in reality. She doubted very much if the lack of invitation would keep him out if he was determined to get in.

She dislodged the unsettling thought by reminding herself she had already decided his threat was an empty one. Nevertheless, she was glad of the work involved in tidying up that kept her busy until lunchtime. The most she could face to eat was a salad, much to Maggie's clucking disapproval, then, still feeling far from settled, she collected her quilted coat from the hall closet and took herself off for a long walk.

She couldn't remember the last time she had had such exercise. Another reminder of how her life had changed. It was a brisk late winter day, the sunshine cheering but without warmth. Yet it was a clean sort of day that made looking to the future hopeful rather than resigned. By the time she had made her way home again, Kate felt invigorated, almost a new person, ready to make drastic changes in her life.

She was making mental plans for a holiday, the first in four hectic years, when her attention was diverted by the sight of a minibus, clearly broken down, not far from the house. Emblazoned on the side was the name of a school, and pressed against the windows were half a dozen curious faces.

With a *frisson* of shock, Kate realised that only days ago she would have walked straight past. For no other reason than that she was too caught up in her own ambitions and she had no time for others. Her footsteps slowed, and she felt a sickening wave of self-disgust. What sort of values were those? The picture she was seeing of herself was appalling. And it was so unlike her—the real Kate—who had somehow got lost when Philip died.

She loved children, had always dreamed of having a large family of her own. Yet she knew she would never have any, and that was a private grief. Something she had accepted years ago. To have children she would have to have a husband, and past experience had shown her that her own inadequacies made that impossible. The hurt was as clear now as if it was only yesterday. She had been so certain of the way her life would go, but fate had had other ideas.

She had dated like any other teenager, but she had experienced none of the excitement her friends talked about. At first she had fought against the knowledge, trying to feel something, even going so far, in a short-lived engagement, to pretend that she did. It had been a fiasco that had finally shown her the truth—that, as a woman, she had something vital lacking.

So she had vowed never to marry. She had accepted, because she had no other choice, that she would never have a husband and family of her own, yet it hadn't stopped her liking children. So to realise she had cut them from her life these last years was a kind of betrayal. Somehow she had to find herself again, and here was the way to start.

With only the briefest hesitation, she walked up to the young woman who appeared to be in charge and who had her head under the raised bonnet.

'Do you need any help?'

The woman straightened, brushing back a riot of auburn curls with a hand that left a greasy streak across her cheek. She looked cheerfully harassed. 'Oh, thank heavens! Do you know anything about engines?'

'I'm afraid not,' Kate admitted ruefully, 'but my house is just over there. You're welcome to use the telephone to get help.' She pointed to where the roof was just visible over the trees, and received a wide smile.

'That's very good of you. The principal will be having kittens by now. I would have walked to the nearest callbox but I couldn't leave the little ones, and they're too tired to walk.'

Kate looked to the window where six faces were peering at her hopefully. The youngest, a little girl with blonde plaits, gave her a gap-toothed grin and Kate felt something tug inside her. She found herself saying, 'If they can manage to walk up to the house, I'm sure we can find some milk and biscuits for them while you make your call.'

The woman looked doubtful. 'I don't want to be any trouble.'

'You won't be,' Kate assured her. 'I'll help you with the children.'

She didn't need more encouragement than that, and quickly organised her charges into pairs on the pavement. Kate felt a tug on her coat and looked down into a pair of large blue eyes. They belonged to the little girl with the plaits.

'I'm tired,' she lisped.

Kate hunkered down, a warm smile softening her features. 'Are you, poppet? I suppose I'd better carry you, then. Come on.' She held out her arms and the little girl went into them, curling her own arms confidingly about Kate's neck. Kate's heart twisted painfully as she stood up, and she realised how much she still wanted a child of her own. The impossibility of it meant there would always be this aching void in her life.

There was a sadness in her eyes as she led the way with that warm bundle in her arms. A half-remembered prayer slipped into her mind: oh, Lord, give me the strength to change what I can, and the grace to accept what I can't. Never had the words been so heartfelt than now, when her life was poised at the crossroads.

If Maggie was surprised by the small invasion party, she said nothing, merely shepherding the small flock into the kitchen where she dispensed milk and biscuits while Kate showed Amy, as the woman had introduced herself, to the telephone. There followed one of the liveliest couple of hours she could remember as they waited for the mechanic to arrive. The children, all orphans, were a lively bunch who soon lost their reserve and embarked on a rowdy game of football on the lawn with a ball Maggie had conjured up from somewhere.

Kate was truly sorry when news came that the minibus was repaired and Amy declared they must go, having imposed themselves on her long enough. Life had come into the house and she was reluctant to abandon it. She helped the younger ones into their coats, knowing her home would seem empty when they were gone, and the one she would miss the most was little Megan. The infant had stayed close to her all the time, chatting away nineteen to the dozen, until she had fallen asleep, and Kate had settled her carefully in an armchair in the sitting-room.

While Amy shepherded the others out to the minibus which had been brought up to the door, Kate went to fetch Megan. It was astounding how quickly she had wormed her way into her heart, she thought, as she picked up the warm armful. Pure instinct had her head lowering, lips brushing a flushed cheek. She straightened with a fond smile, easing damp curls away from the smooth forehead. Then the sensation of being watched made her tense and turn her head swiftly to the door.

Kate's heart thudded at the shock of finding Aidan Crawford's tall figure filling the doorway. A vastly different-looking man from the one she had seen last night. In jeans, Argyll sweater and black leather jacket, he looked no less powerful and threatening, yet more ruggedly handsome, and with an animal magnetism that even she couldn't be unaware of. A trickle of sensation traced its way up and down her spine.

She stiffened automatically, at once made uncomfortably aware of her make-up-free face, mussed hair, and the child in her arms. She paled, skin tightening, and then hot colour rose in her cheeks as she saw on his face an expression somewhat akin to shock. It was replaced in quick succession by disbelief and anger before, spine stiffening, he wiped his face clean. Yet there was a peculiar tension in the air that made her swallow to

moisten a suddenly dry mouth. For a moment, silence
reigned as they simply stared at each other.

'A young woman outside told me to come in,' he broke
the silence in a voice that sounded gravelly and tight.

Amy, Kate thought with a groan, knowing the other
woman could have no idea how unwelcome this visitor
was, especially if he had made it sound as if he was
expected. How she hated to be caught at a disadvantage
like this. More so when she had not expected to see him
again. Consequently her tone was at once defensive and
peremptory.

'What do you want?'

His only reaction was a slight narrowing of the eyes.
'To talk to you. I said I'd be back,' he reminded her.

There was no sense in telling him she hadn't taken him
seriously. She had fallen into the oldest trap of underestimating her opponent, and now here he was, and she
was in no shape to cope with him. She had hardly come
to terms with the new person inside her; certainly it was
no time to put it to the test with Aidan Crawford.

She was about to send him on his way in short order
when the bundle in her arms stirred.

'That hurts, Auntie Kate,' Megan protested, and Kate
realised she had been squeezing the child unconsciously.

Contrite, she forced herself to relax and dropped a
quick kiss on the little girl's cheek. 'Sorry, sweetheart.
Come along, I'm going to take you out to Amy now.'
She looked up at Aidan Crawford and discovered him
watching her with an intensity that was disconcerting.
'You'd better wait here,' she suggested ungraciously, and
he nodded and stepped aside.

Kate went past him, expelling a breath she hadn't
realised she was holding. She had the crazy feeling she'd
just escaped—but from what, she couldn't say. She didn't
like the way he set her nerves on edge, and the sooner
he left again, the better.

It was the work of a moment to carry Megan outside and pass her on to Amy, who was voluble in her thanks, and once again apologising for the trouble they had caused. There followed a noisy departure with much calling and waving that she returned until a turn in the drive took the minibus from her view behind the shrubbery. Her hand dropped to her side, and the smile died on her lips as the quiet descended once more, leaving only echoes in the mind.

To take her thoughts from the path they wanted to tread, she turned them to Aidan Crawford as she reluctantly faced the house. Why had he had to turn up now, of all times? Shivering, she tried to rub warmth into her arms. His presence made her feel vulnerable all at once. So much so, that, when she did make her way slowly back into the sitting-room, she was even more stiffly defensive.

He was standing with his back to the window, but she didn't doubt for a moment that he had watched the scene outside. She was aware of a surge of anger. She didn't want him invading her privacy like this. She wasn't ready, caught as she was in the middle of a painful rebirth. And because the fledgeling Kate couldn't hope to cope, she summoned up remnants of the old Kate to face him.

'The children seem to like you,' he observed, making no effort to hide his surprise.

She bridled instantly. 'I happen to like them, too,' she informed him tartly.

That raised an eyebrow indicative of scepticism. 'Do you keep it hidden because it doesn't go with your image?' There was just enough mockery in his tone to set her teeth on edge.

'I keep it private because it is just that.' Or would have been until *he* burst in on it uninvited.

'If you value your privacy so much, why allow children in?' he asked curiously.

It would have been simple to say she needed them, but an imp of perversity made her tilt her chin at him instead. 'Perhaps I enjoy playing Lady Bountiful,' she rejoined sweetly.

To her surprise he thought about that for some seconds, then shook his head. What he said next took the ground from under her feet. 'I might have believed it if I hadn't seen your reaction to the little girl. No one can fake affection, and children pick it up more quickly than adults. Which makes me wonder why you don't have children of your own.'

The casual question speared her heart with a pain so keen that she couldn't hide a small gasp. His perception was frightening. No one else had seen so much in so short a time. She tried to smile, knew she had failed, and turned away, masking her discomposure by crossing quickly to the small selection of drinks set up on a tray on the sideboard. She felt queer and shaky inside, and wondered what was the matter with her. Whatever it was, she was determined he shouldn't see it. Still with her back turned, she produced a falsely bright laugh and shrugged.

'I've been too busy, I suppose. But maybe one day I will do just that,' she lied, dropping her lids over smarting eyes. She sought for control and finally found it. 'Can I get you a drink?' Good old Kate, she thought, slipping into her role gratefully, and turned to face him enquiringly.

'Not for me, thanks. It's a little early,' Aidan Crawford declined smoothly, but his gaze was narrowed and watchful.

Fearing he had seen too much, Kate hurried on. 'What did you want to see me about?' She was proud of the coolness of her tone, especially when she thought she could guess. She hadn't forgotten his threat.

'I went to see Julia today.'

She raised her brows even as a pang of guilt smote her. She had been trying not to think of his bride-to-be. The effects of her actions yesterday were spreading like ripples on a pond. 'Naturally I assumed you would. However I don't see what that has to do with me.'

'I know you don't, but you will.' The promise was edged. Her offhand tone had annoyed him. 'Julia, my dear Kate, was still bloody furious,' he informed her succinctly.

He didn't need to try and make her feel guilty, she'd already accepted her culpability. 'But surely you told her the truth?'

'But surely,' he mimicked right back, 'you didn't expect her to believe me?'

That gave her pause, because initially the possibility must have been in the back of her mind. Since learning of her mistake she had assumed... clearly too much. Another rush of guilt made her frown, and conversely her tone became light, almost frivolous. 'She's upset. I'm sure if she loves you she'll——'

Aidan Crawford broke in abruptly. 'I see that amuses you. Perhaps this will, too. Julia doesn't love me; she never did.'

Kate actually found herself shocked into silence. Everything she had planned was happening, only now, of course, she didn't want it to. A rather reluctant sympathy for him was roused. The only platitude that came to mind was that, better he should find out now about the fickleness of his fiancée than later. She began to say as much.

'I'm sorry——'

'Don't be. Neither did I love her. What we had was a mutual understanding.'

The sheer cold-bloodedness of the way he spoke of an institution she had always held sacred rapidly dispelled her sympathy. Her lip curled in a way that many a man would have recognised with dismay. 'In that case, there's no reason why you can't still be married,' she returned witheringly. They sounded as if they deserved each other.

Aidan Crawford laughed, but not with humour. 'Ah, but then you don't know Julia. There's every reason. Julia abhors scandal. She especially dislikes being made a laughing stock.' He spoke as if he were repeating her word for word. 'Her pride wouldn't let her contemplate marrying me now.'

Dear heaven, and these were the people who had caused her to change her life! She was disgusted. 'I'm sure you can find a replacement, given time. Love being surplus to requirements!' she mocked.

He turned away then, to stare out of the window, hands sliding into his pockets. 'As you say, love being unnecessary, I'm sure I could, but time is something I don't have.' Once again his brief laugh was mirthless, almost as if the joke, if there was one, was on him.

Kate shrugged, ignoring a tweak of intrigue. 'That's your problem. I don't know what you expect me to do.'

He turned round again, grey eyes glinting. 'What I expect you to do, *Ms* Hardie, is quite simple...and is something only you can do.'

There was something in his tone that had the fine hairs rising all over her body. She found herself staring at him as if mesmerised. His voice was perfectly level as he went on, and he never once took his eyes off her.

'I need a wife. But for you I would have had one. I don't have time to look for another, and I don't believe I need to. You elected yourself my wife yesterday, and I'm holding you to that. You owe me, Kate Hardie, and I'm collecting on the debt.'

They faced each other across the cosy room which had suddenly become an arena.

'You can't be serious!' From somewhere Kate managed to find her voice.

'I've never been more so,' he promised shortly.

'Then you're mad. Totally and utterly mad!' She tried to laugh, but the look on his face, the determination, was quelling. Her heart began to thud. He meant it!

'No, not mad. Just playing the game with the cards I've been dealt,' he declared forcefully.

Yet underneath the anger, the new Kate detected a note of...surely it couldn't be desperation? Except there was a certain tension in him that went beyond anger, finding an outlet in the frustrated way he dragged a hand through his hair. It stopped her on the verge of an outright no.

Curiosity got the better of her. 'Why?'

His mouth drew into a thin line. 'The why comes later, after you've agreed to marry me,' he told her grimly.

A laugh was forced out of her at his sheer arrogance. 'You're crazy if you expect any woman to make that sort of leap in the dark!' She threw up a hand in disbelief. 'And just why should I agree to marry the man who...who...?' She faltered to a halt as she realised what she was saying.

His thoughts were there ahead of her, and there was a tight smile on his lips. 'Who did nothing to you. Who would have helped your brother if he had known in time. The man whom, by your own admission, you set out to destroy yesterday. If you need a why, there's a simple one. Moral obligation.'

Kate paled. Every word he shot at her was true. She was ready to admit that, but not that he had come to the wrong person. How could she say that she couldn't help even if she wanted to? He was asking the impossible—the one thing she couldn't do. It set her at odds with herself and made her feel uncomfortably vulnerable. She didn't like that, and quickly summoned up the old image to protect herself.

'I'll admit I was in the wrong, Mr Crawford, but marriage isn't part of my plans. You'll have to look elsewhere,' she told him shortly.

He made a move towards her, controlled it, and crossed his arms. 'I've already told you there's no time. I'm not asking for a lifetime commitment. All I need is a wife for a limited time.'

Kate hesitated. She was the last person he'd choose unless he had no option. So whatever it was must be important. She was to blame and certainly owed him. But could she live with this man in a temporary marriage that was more like a business deal? She looked at him, and knew she couldn't. But for the scar, he was Andrew Crawford—a constant reminder of Philip. No! It was impossible. Even a day would be too long!

'No. I'm sorry. Long or short, it's out of the question,' she refused huskily. 'If I wanted a husband at all, believe me, I would never pick you.'

Something flashed in his eyes. 'Damn it! Do you think that given a choice I would ever pick you? A woman who's cold and vindictive? Who treats men with such icy contempt? Oh, no. I'd choose a woman who's that in every sense of the word. One who's warm and responsive, loving and giving—none of which qualities you possess the smallest fraction of. A man wants a real woman in his bed, Kate, not an Ice Queen with nothing to give!'

Pale as a ghost, she stared at him as each word struck home in her heart with carelessly brutal accuracy. There wasn't a part of her that didn't tremble. Not even the old Kate, fully in control, could have withstood that bombardment. Tears she had thought she was long past shedding glittered in her eyes. When he had finished, she swallowed painfully.

'You don't understand!' she protested, the words breaking from her unbidden. The minute she watched his lips curl she wished them unsaid.

'On the contrary, I understand you only too well. You've no heart, and for that I pity you.'

To have him pity her was too much. 'What a lucky escape for you, then, that I said no!' she jeered, but her voice broke on the last and she turned her back on him abruptly.

The silence that fell was thick with seething emotions. Into it Aidan Crawford's surprised voice said questioningly, 'Kate?'

It fired her to face him once more, chin lifted proudly. Only the brilliance of her eyes gave anything away. 'I think we've both said more than enough, don't you? I won't change my mind, so you'd only be wasting your time. In which case, I think you should leave.'

For one tense moment, she thought he was about to argue, that he was going to follow up the curiosity her reaction had aroused. But her mask was back in place now, giving the lie to that instant of vulnerability, and she saw the moment when he shrugged mentally and decided he must have imagined it.

Without another word he crossed to the door, but instead of going through it he paused to look back at her. The contempt in his eyes was chilling, and Kate braced herself.

'Damn you, Kate Hardie. I hope you can live with yourself,' he flung at her bitterly, and then he did go, crashing the front door behind him, making her flinch.

Shivering in reaction, Kate hugged her arms around herself. He had gone, and this time she knew he wasn't coming back. Her lips twisted. Who would want to return to someone who wasn't a real woman? Immediately she was disgusted with the lapse into self-pity. Damn him. He had got through her defences like a hot knife through butter. With accusations that had been levelled at her before, but never with such success.

They hurt. All the more because they weren't true. For four years she might have behaved as if a softer side didn't exist, but it did, and now she was reaping the result of the image she had created. It was too painful. She didn't want to feel like this. For a moment she wanted the old Kate back, but knew that that person could never be complete again. The mirage might defend her, but it could never stop the hurt. In one night she had changed too much, gone too far down a new and untravelled road. There was no going back.

It wasn't going to be easy facing the world without her shell, but at least she wouldn't have to see Aidan Crawford again. That cold-blooded marriage he had planned was horrible, putting him on a par with his brother. Anger stirred her, and she whipped it up. They used people. Used them for their own ends. She was glad she'd said no, her guilty conscience subdued by his mercenary behaviour. She hadn't destroyed anything of value. He had as good as told her that. So she had no reason at all to feel guilty!

Furthermore, the Crawfords were out of her life for good, and that was exactly the way she wanted it.

CHAPTER FOUR

UNFORTUNATELY, the past had a way of rearing its head, but Kate wasn't thinking of that as she prepared the following Sunday evening for a charity gala. She had been committed to going months ago, so there was no getting out of it, which was what she felt like. However, she was used to putting on a bright face, and at least the cause was a worthy one.

A greater part of her reluctance was due to the fact that Jonathan Carteret was to be her escort. As she took a leisurely bath, her thoughts turned to him. Jonathan presented a new dilemma. She had treated him shabbily because he was becoming too persistent, much too intense. He would still have to go, but the trouble was the new Kate couldn't reconcile herself to treating him as cavalierly as the old Kate would have done. She didn't want to hurt him any more than she already had.

She sighed as she reached for the sponge and soap. This past week had been an experience she wouldn't want to undergo again. Her attempts to soften her ways had been met with deep suspicion which had stung. But she hadn't given up, and had reached Friday with the knowledge that her colleagues had stopped laughing and were prepared to give her the benefit of the doubt.

But that still left the problem of Jonathan. Rediscovering her conscience was painful, bringing ghosts to haunt her. Climbing out of the cooling water and wrapping herself in a large fluffy bathsheet, Kate pulled a wry face. If Aidan Crawford could see her mental agonies, how he would enjoy it! Damn! She must stop thinking about him. His parting words had taunted her all week, much to her discomfort.

Once again she determinedly pushed him to the back of her mind, hoping that this time he would stay there, and got on with the business of dressing. As a rule, she enjoyed deciding what to wear for maximum effect, but tonight it wasn't surprising that her mind wasn't really on it. Even so, surveying the end result critically, she knew she looked her best with her hair swept up, and the strapless blue taffeta evening dress rustling enticingly as she walked. The diamonds at her ears and throat were real, but the fur cape Jonathan slipped about her shoulders before they left the house was not. She believed passionately that fur looked best where it belonged—on the animal.

The Opera House was ablaze with lights and buzzing with excited voices. Everyone who was anyone was present, the ladies' jewels and dresses adding to the glittering occasion. Their progress to their box was slow. Every few yards there was a friend to exchange greetings with. Only the severest control and the full recourse of her training stopped Kate from doing what she wanted to do, which was escape from the throng and get a moment's peace. By the time they did reach their seats, her nerves were distinctly brittle, the muscles of her face aching from smiling constantly.

Kate took her seat with a sigh. She hadn't been looking forward to the evening, but at that stage she didn't know it was to turn into one she would never forget.

The selections from opera and ballet failed to completely hold her attention, though many were her favourites. She had too much on her mind. Jonathan's constant attentions to her every need, which once she would have accepted disdainfully, made her feel uncomfortable, and not a little embarrassed. His dog-like devotion was demeaning, and knowing she was entirely responsible made her despise herself.

Consequently, she felt snappy and irritable when the interval came, and when Jonathan asked her if she was quite comfortable for the nth time, she exploded nervously.

'Oh, for goodness' sake, Jonathan, do shut up!'

For the first time she saw a mutinous look on his amiable face. 'I don't suppose you'd talk to him like that,' he said curtly.

Surprised, Kate blinked. 'Him—who?'

Jonathan's laugh was bitter. 'Who, she says! Macho man with the strong arm tactics, that's who. I didn't see you putting up much of a fight the other night. I've always respected you, Kate. You should have told me that wasn't what you wanted.'

Kate could only stare at him, stunned at the swiftness with which the worm had turned. Of course, she knew who he meant, but his interpretation of what he had witnessed shocked her. 'If you think I enjoyed that, you were mistaken. I didn't protest because I didn't want to cause a scene.'

'I'll bet!' he sneered, all sign of mild manners gone. 'Just what went on in there, Kate? He didn't look the type to ask permission. He's the sort who takes what he wants. And what about you, Kate, did you enjoy it?'

She was too stunned to make any sort of denial, and could only exclaim helplessly, 'Jonathan, this isn't like you!'

He stood up jerkily. 'How would you know? You've never looked at me long enough to find out!'

Which was true. She'd only seen a docile lap-dog, not the human being she'd used. 'I'm sorry,' she apologised softly, attempting to mollify, an art she was out of practice with. 'You're right. I've behaved badly. We should talk, but this isn't the time or place. Later. I...have something important to say to you.'

Jonathan laughed harshly. 'Let me guess what it is! And to think I thought you were special! I'm going to the bar. Do you want anything?'

Kate winced. It wasn't the most gracious of offers, but she knew better now than to try and laugh it off. 'Thank you, I'd love a glass of water.'

'With ice, naturally,' he added pithily, the perfect parting shot. The door closed behind him with a decided click.

Kate subsided with a shaken breath. She'd never seen Jonathan in such a mood, and she had to admit it made her uneasy. She had hoped to break with him in a dignified way; now she wasn't so certain that would be possible.

A soft tap on the door interrupted her thoughts, and she looked around quickly, aware that it was too soon for Jonathan to have returned. She was right. The man who came in bore no resemblance to her escort. Kate felt fatalistic. It didn't surprise her at all that Aidan Crawford should turn up to haunt her. It was turning out to be that sort of week. She refused to look away from him, for she had nothing to fear. But as he came closer to her, her eyes registered a disturbing fact. His face bore no scar!

Kate paled with the shock of it. For this wasn't Aidan Crawford but Andrew who stood before her. He was exactly as she remembered him. She wondered how she could ever have mistaken Aidan for him. They were alike, yet so unlike. Grey eyes looked out at her from the handsome face, assessing and coveting. How could she have forgotten them? Or the overly sensual lips that spoke of a corrupt life of indulgence. His crocodile smile very nearly made her shudder.

Her reaction was alarming and totally unexpected. A cold, sick dread settled in her stomach. The hairs on the back of her neck rose atavistically, and suddenly she was finding it difficult to breathe. A corner of her mind registered the signs of anxiety, and though she couldn't say why she knew she was afraid of this man. Every instinct she possessed was urging her to run, yet, of all the things she had learnt over the years, to show nothing of what she was feeling was by far the most important now.

He took Jonathan's seat and relaxed back, crossing his legs. The grey gaze he ran over her was possessive, noting the agitated rise and fall of her breasts. 'Kate,' he greeted her, her name slipping off his tongue reminiscently.

Until it happened she had never thought it could, but her flesh actually crawled. She could sense that inexplicable fear growing, trying to take over, and she fought it down. He was trying to unsettle her, but he was going to fail. It took all her will-power to slow her pulse rate down to near normal. 'Andrew,' she returned smoothly, hiding her revulsion. Never had the Ice Queen persona been more necessary.

In reply he threw back his head and laughed. 'So, you've met my estimable brother at last. Darling, you were perfect. I don't think I'll ever forget that marvellous scene in the church.'

At the endearment Kate's nerves jolted badly and her stomach turned over. 'You were there?' She saved her composure by a whisker, but the effort tensed every nerve and muscle.

'Of course. I am family, you know,' he laughed again. 'You should have stayed longer. Aidan was almost beside himself, and Julia was throwing a fit. I couldn't have planned anything better if I'd tried.'

Oh, God! She experienced a savage impulse to claw that satisfied smirk from his face and reveal him for the vermin he was! She felt contaminated just at being near him. Yet she allowed nothing to show on her face. 'I didn't see you.' If she had, how different things might have been.

'I know. You had eyes for one man only. But I saw you, Kate. You've come a long way since we first met. You've grown more beautiful.'

The compliment made her want to be sick, and deep inside an insidious trembling began. 'I've certainly grown older...and wiser,' she admitted.

Andrew Crawford smiled. 'But no less impulsive. How well I remember that impulsiveness! Of course, as soon as I saw you, I knew what you were doing. It's a pity you didn't get your revenge. I appreciated your initiative, though I doubt anyone else did.'

'I *so* glad it amused you,' Kate rejoined sarcastically, while her mind assimilated his words. What did he mean—her impulsiveness?

'Now, now, don't be bitter. You should have known you couldn't beat me.'

'I couldn't beat you if I didn't know you existed. But I do now,' Kate observed coolly, wishing him gone. Feeling oppressed by the thickening atmosphere.

Andrew Crawford shook his head. 'Ah, Kate, that's no way to talk. Besides, you can't annoy me when I'm celebrating Aidan's downfall.'

The antipathy he obviously felt for his brother was incomprehensible to Kate. 'What did he ever do to you?'

Not for an instant did the smiling mask slip. 'He exists, isn't that enough?' he answered simply. 'But he wishes he didn't—and all because of you, Kate. I guessed you'd be here tonight, so I came to commiserate with you. A nice try, but I'm too clever for you. Still, that shouldn't stop you from joining in my little celebration.'

His vanity was breathtaking! 'Oughtn't I to know exactly what it is you're celebrating?' Somehow, an intensely feminine instinct overrode her disgust, telling her that this was important. Andrew Crawford had come to gloat, and not just about his victory over herself. Whatever it was, his vanity made an audience a necessary part of his enjoyment.

'I was only waiting for you to ask. My dear brother Aidan is about to lose a fortune. You've no doubt heard of Cranston Electronics? It was started by our maternal grandfather after the last war, but it was Aidan who built it up into a worldwide concern. He was tipped to succeed old Cranston as chairman when he retired, and that happened about six years ago. Now Aidan was always his blue-eyed boy, but there was one thing they never could agree on. The old man wanted him to marry and my brother always refused. They had some monumental rows about it, the last of which I was privy to. Grandfather told Aidan that unless he married before his thirty-eighth birthday he would be written out of his will. That didn't mean just money, but company shares too, the controlling interest would go elsewhere.

'To cut a long story short, Grandfather died just under two months ago, and not two weeks later Aidan announced his engagement. A month later and the wedding almost took place. Now that almost seems like indecent haste to me. It didn't take a genius to realise the old man had done what he said he would and poor Aidan had been brought to heel after all. He would have won it, too, if it hadn't been for you.'

Kate was left absolutely speechless with disgust. This man wasn't human! His sheer vindictiveness and spite sickened her.

'The beauty of it,' Andrew Crawford continued, 'is that I didn't have to do a thing.'

No, Kate thought, I did it for you. What else have you done to him without ever getting your slimy hands dirty? You're sick and evil, and I can't even pity you. She had had enough. She had to get away—right away to where she could breathe clean, fresh air. Even as the wish came, the means of achieving it arrived. Jonathan walked in, halting abruptly when he saw she was not alone. Recognition of her companion sent him rigid as he held out the glass he brought with him.

'Your drink, Kate.' His voice was clipped and angry.

She knew what he was thinking, but didn't bother to disabuse him. There was an angry sparkle in her eye as she smiled her thanks and claimed the glass.

'Lovely, Jonathan, I've been waiting for this,' she declared, and in the next instant had thrown the contents full in Andrew Crawford's face.

The smile was extinguished like a flame, leaving behind a dripping glare as he shot to his feet. 'Bitch! I'll make you sorry for that.'

Perhaps he would, but Kate didn't care. She was too angry and disgusted and only wanted to get out of there. She ignored him and turned to the astonished man at her side.

'Take me home, Jonathan,' she commanded, rising quickly, leaving the box as fast as her legs would allow.

'What was that all about?' Jonathan asked as he caught up with her in the corridor with her cape.

Shuddering, Kate pulled the folds around her. She was trembling so badly that only her anger kept one foot in front of the other. 'You don't want to know. Believe me, you don't want to know.'

'It's that man,' he persisted belligerently. 'What is he to you, Kate?'

Kate turned on him impatiently. Couldn't he see this was the wrong time and place? 'He's nothing to me. *No* man is anything to me, Jonathan,' she finished, far more pointedly than she had intended, and caught her lip between her teeth in dismay as he stiffened.

'I see. Well, that certainly puts *me* in my place, doesn't it. They were right, weren't they, all those others? You just use men.'

She winced. This wasn't the way she had wanted it to be. Instinctively she placed her hand on his arm. 'Jonathan——' she began falteringly, only to have him shrug her off distastefully.

'I got the message already. You'll have to find someone else to lead around by the nose. I'll see you home, but there's no point in our seeing each other again.'

Kate couldn't blame him for taking out his anger on her—she deserved it. She had handled the situation very badly from start to finish. 'I'll get a taxi,' she said quickly, wanting only a speedy end to another disastrous evening.

'I was brought up with the good manners to make sure my partner arrived safely home after a date whatever the circumstances,' he contradicted her, and stood aside stiffly for a quelled Kate to lead the way out.

The journey home was silent. Neither of them had anything to say. Jonathan escorted her right to the door like the perfect gentleman he was, bade her a curt goodnight and walked out of her life with his dignity intact.

Quashed, Kate let herself into the house and made straight for the lounge, switching on lights as she went. She wasn't much of a drinker, but she needed the brandy she poured for herself just then. The tremble in her hand was proof enough, and she drank it down quickly. It started a warmth in her stomach that gradually steadied her limbs. No man had ever made her feel afraid simply by his presence the way Andrew Crawford had. It was inexplicable, but it had been very real, and she was still unnerved. She knew she should hate him, but not why she should react the way she had. And why, if she felt that with him, wasn't it the same with his brother? It made no sense—it simply was, and she was angry with herself for being upset by it.

She couldn't get out of her mind the picture of Andrew Crawford's gloating face as he told her of his brother. It was all a game to him, and he didn't care who got hurt in the process, so long as he won.

With a cry of disgust, Kate flung the empty glass into the grate where it shattered into a thousand pieces.

'Damn you, Andrew Crawford! Damn your loathsome soul for winning again!'

He had used her to beat his brother even as he beat her, and now he was beating them both. Her impotent anger soared, then dived into despair. But only for a moment.

'No!' The fiercely defiant word echoed around the room as her pride surged anew. 'No,' she said again. She was too angry to despair, too sickened with disgust. She *would* not let him win.

Tonight Andrew Crawford had made a mistake. He had crowed too soon, and to the wrong woman. He had overreached himself, for he knew nothing of her meetings with his brother. He had gloated, wanting to make her suffer even as his brother was, but all he had succeeded in doing was making her angry. So angry it was like a volcano inside her, looking for a way out.

Now she understood Aidan Crawford's anger and frustration. Why hadn't he told her about the will? Stupid, she already knew the answer. Why should he reveal his most private problems to a woman who had helped to destroy him? He couldn't be expected to know that he would be appealing to her own sense of morality. He didn't believe she had one!

But he was going to find out differently, because to-night his brother had made her angry enough to cast aside all caution and do the one thing she had never thought to do—marry Aidan Crawford.

It was no longer a matter of owing him, or of seeking revenge. It was simply doing the right thing. She knew she would never forgive herself if she did nothing, for it was a matter of principle. She had it in her power to do right where wrong was intended. Personal feelings no longer came into it. They could be put aside.

With her mind made up, Kate wasted no time. Going through to her study, she reached for the telephone directory, found the number she wanted, and punched it out firmly. At the other end, the phone rang and rang. Kate wondered if he was asleep, but shrugged off any feelings of dismay. For this call, Aidan Crawford wouldn't mind being roused from his bed. Finally, just as she was about to give up, the receiver was lifted.

'Crawford here,' a well-remembered voice snapped irritably.

The sound of it made Kate shiver. She took a deep breath. 'Mr Crawford, this is Kate Hardie. I've changed my mind. If you still need a wife, I'll marry you,' she declared coolly, even as her heart gave a wild panicky leap.

There was silence for perhaps ten seconds, and when he spoke his tone had altered dramatically. 'I'll be right over,' he stated equally coolly, and the receiver went back down, cutting them off.

Kate stared at the lifeless instrument in her hand and slowly lowered it to the rest. She had an overwhelming sense of having burnt her boats. She had just agreed to marry the brother of the man who had ruined her life— and it felt as though the limb she had climbed out on could barely support her weight. More, he was on his way over right now. She hadn't bargained on that.

She glanced down at her evening dress. She would have to change. She couldn't meet him dressed so—Ice

Queenishly. God, how she was coming to loathe that name. The anger that had carried her this far began to evaporate. She prayed she was doing the right thing, but she had given her word, and that had always been her bond.

Swallowing down a sense of panic, she went up to change.

The doorbell rang as Kate was making her way downstairs, and she went to answer it with a distinct feeling of trepidation. This meeting was going to be a test of character. While changing she had debated what line to take. They were hardly on the best of terms, but she would rather they were a little friendlier to make the task ahead of them easier. So she had decided to abandon the persona he hated so much and meet him on new ground, showing him that she did have a softer side.

Aidan Crawford stepped inside without waiting to be invited, making the well-proportioned hall shrink in size by the sheer vibrancy of his presence. She was very much aware of his narrow-eyed regard as she closed the door, and was glad she had changed into the peacock-blue mohair sweater and cream trousers. She could imagine his remarks if she had met him in all her finery! Especially as he was dressed very much as she had seen him that other afternoon.

She turned to him at last and tried to find a faint smile, but her face was far too tight with stress. 'There was no need to rush over, you know.'

He looked at her levelly. 'I disagree. You probably have a habit of changing your mind as often as you do your men. I wanted to get here while the mood was still on you.'

Kate paled, her heart sinking at his attitude. Naïvely, she realised, she had expected gratitude. Clearly a mistake. 'Mood?' She clamped her hands together be-

cause they showed a distinct tendency to tremble, and
she was loath to let him see she wasn't in total control.

'Of regal beneficence. I'd be interested to know what
happened to make you decide to repay your debt to this
lesser mortal,' he drawled sarcastically.

In a flash the old Kate had resurrected herself. 'I might
tell you if you stop insulting me long enough!'

Far from being rebuked, he only smiled. 'They do say,
if you can't take it, don't dish it out.'

That brought swift colour to her cheeks. 'Perhaps they
do, but *they* don't need a wife in a hurry,' she told him
pointedly. 'Are you deliberately trying to make me
change my mind?' she demanded to know. If he was,
he was doing a grand job of it!

Aidan Crawford inclined his head. 'My apologies. I
had no idea you were so...sensitive.'

It took an effort, but Kate ignored that goad. It wasn't
a very auspicious start, but she wasn't giving up yet. She
must stop letting him get to her. 'Let's go into the sitting-
room,' she suggested, and led the way. She took the seat
she had occupied last night and watched as he settled
himself in the chair opposite. 'Would you like coffee? I
can soon make some,' she offered politely, but he shook
his head.

'Not right now, thanks,' he declined, and fixed his
grey glance on her pale face. 'So, you'll marry me. Why
the sudden change of heart?'

She had known he would ask that question, and had
decided, as she changed, that the truth was probably the
best answer.

'I met your brother tonight. He was...celebrating.'
There was no way she could hide her revulsion at the
memory. She glanced at her companion and found he
had gone quite still. Yet to her mind he seemed to be
bracing himself, waiting for something he knew he
wouldn't like.

'Celebrating?'

It was as if the softer Kate was tuned in to a new level of awareness. Ultra-sensitive to invisible undercurrents, she sensed that, although he didn't show it, he was in pain from an old wound, and that what she had to say would tear it open again. She knew, as surely as if he had told her, that he loved his brother despite everything, and the wounds of receiving only hatred in return were bitter. The thought of inflicting more pain was contrary to a nature she had thought buried long ago. But it, too, was still there, dormant but not dead. She wished she could avoid the next few seconds for his sake, but he had to know.

'Actually, he came to gloat,' she explained, feeling her way.

'Go on,' he encouraged hardily.

Kate licked her lips nervously. 'At first I thought it was just over my mistaking you for him, but that wasn't all. He...thanked me for ruining the wedding, because it meant you would lose control of Cranston's.' She stopped because it was hard to go on when he had paled so much that the scar stood out vividly on his cheek.

She felt helpless, stirred by an inexplicable urge to offer him some comfort, and not knowing how to handle the startling revelation of the feeling. It brought a bubble of hysteria to her chest. Not only did he not look the sort of man you would give comfort to, but even if he was, she wasn't the woman he would accept it from. The very thought was crazy—she was crazy!

She cleared her throat abruptly. 'You should have told me about the will.'

'The will!' he declared harshly, then left his chair to stalk to the window, staring out into the darkness. 'Just what the hell has Andrew been saying?' He threw the question at her over his shoulder.

'That your grandfather had cut you out of his will unless you married, and that you'd lose control of the business,' she told his rigid back, seeing the way he squared his shoulders as he listened.

'I see. So that's it,' he said flatly.

'You should have told me,' Kate repeated.

'The company is my business,' he stated firmly.

Kate stared at his uncompromising back. 'You tried to make it mine,' she reminded him.

He turned round at that. 'Are you saying that if I had told you this last week, you would have agreed then?'

The grey eyes seemed to bore into her, and she was forced to drop hers. 'I'm...not sure,' she answered huskily, and that was the truth. Without the extra goad of Andrew Crawford's delight, would she have had the nerve to do this?

His brother seemed to have no such doubts. 'Don't try to kid yourself, Kate. You aren't doing this for the company or me, but for yourself. You still want your revenge,' he told her bluntly, and Kate came to her feet, stirred by the small grain of truth in what he said. She was human, and the old Kate couldn't be wiped out that quickly.

She dragged a hand through her hair. 'Perhaps I do, but so much has happened, I'm not sure of anything any more. All I do know is that I won't let your brother win again. You want your company, and I'm prepared to do my best to help you get it. Why I'm doing it really doesn't matter in the long run, does it?' she challenged.

A curious expression crossed his face for a moment before it closed up. 'That's the question, isn't it? I happen to think it does. I love my brother, Kate. I'm not about to stand by while you try to hurt him.'

Kate gave a broken laugh. 'That's crazy. He's the one who's hurting you. He hates you.'

He came back to her then. 'And because of that, do you think I should hate him in return? I'm afraid it doesn't work that way.'

'My brother, right or wrong?' she jeered.

His eyes narrowed angrily. 'I can't—won't—change the way I feel.'

'And he knows it, and hates you all the more for it,' Kate exclaimed in disbelief.

Aidan Crawford's expression remained stony. 'I meant what I said, Kate. I won't have him hurt. I won't have you playing your tricks on him.'

She withdrew into herself at once, remembering that inexplicable fear. 'There's no danger of that,' she returned frigidly. 'Believe it or not, I don't want to hurt your brother—even should such a thing be possible, which I doubt. All I intend to do is stop him from using me to hurt you,' she protested strongly, willing him to accept what she knew to be the truth.

'And so you nobly agreed to marry me,' he drawled cynically.

'Yes,' Kate concurred shortly, 'but there are conditions.'

A mocking smile twisted his lips. 'Naturally. I wouldn't expect you to do this for nothing.'

Kate's teeth came together in a snap. 'I don't want your money. I have more than enough of my own. I meant that I will only marry you on the strict understanding that the marriage is one of convenience.' There was a sound basis why she needed his agreement. She saw no good reason for holding her own inadequacies up to his ridicule for what was to be only a temporary marriage. He had enough weapons already without stripping her pride away, too. If he objected, then the deal was off. She didn't wait long for his answer.

'That, my dear Kate, is the only type of marriage I'd be prepared to undergo with you,' he whipped back smartly.

There was absolutely no reason why his words should strike home so sharply, but, like so much else he had said, they found her vulnerable spot with an accuracy that was frightening. And because she didn't know how to handle it she hid her reaction behind a surge of anger that was pure Ice Queen.

'There's no need to be so insulting. After all, I'm doing *you* the favour, remember.'

His look was every bit as chilling as hers. 'So you are, but let's get something straight right now. The Ice Queen image doesn't impress me one jot. I'm not about to start grovelling to you. If that's what you expect, then thanks, but no, thanks,' he concluded cuttingly.

Kate blanched. Nobody spoke to her like that! Not with such searing contempt. 'How dare you?' she choked. 'What sort of woman do you take me for?'

Aidan Crawford lifted his hand and caught hold of her chin in a relentless grip that she immediately fought against but in vain. Inside her chest, her heart started a frantic beating as he gave her a long searching look before replying. 'I take you to be what I now know you to be. I haven't been idle. I've been learning *all* about you. Kate Hardie, the eternal virgin. Reeling men in with the promise of your sensuality. Making them your slaves so that they'd do anything for the chance of breaking into the citadel you guard so jealously. And when their antics cease to amuse, when they bore you, you drop them, don't you, Kate? No man will ever break down the wall because you won't let them. No man could love you more than you love yourself. No man could do you justice. So you remain inviolate and scorn the fools who break themselves against your walls.'

Horrified by the picture he painted, Kate couldn't unlock her gaze from his. It was a scathing indictment that made her shrivel up inside, because it had been ninety-nine per cent true less than forty-eight hours ago.

'That's...horrible,' she gasped, her heart beating achingly fast.

'The truth often is,' he agreed chillingly. 'But be warned, Kate. I'm not like any man you've ever met before. I don't ask, or plead, or grovel. I don't play by your rules, only my own.' His voice dropped to a husky growl. 'I take what I want. Like this...'

Before she had a chance to do more than register the shock of his intent, his head had swooped and his lips claimed hers. Automatically Kate froze. Then every nerve in her body shattered like glass as something resembling an electric shock went through her. All concept of what a kiss could be was exploded by that searing touch. The heat from his lips sent her blood rushing crazily along her veins and she couldn't move as his kiss forced her head back, ravishing her mouth. Her body became an alien thing she didn't recognise as for the first time it responded to a call as old as time itself. Dizzily, she felt her bones dissolve, her flesh quickening, as tiny flames of pleasure burst like fireworks inside her. Nothing had prepared her for this intense excitement as the kiss went on and on. Overwhelmed, she trembled and a moan forced its way from her throat as she unconsciously swayed towards him.

As if that was the sign he had been waiting for, he lifted his head at last and looked down into blue eyes darkened by conflicting emotions, his own hooded and watchful. From somewhere Kate found the strength to pull herself free of his touch, vitally aware that her body was telling her it didn't want to move. It wanted to press closer, experience again that strange new excitement. With a shudder of pure shock, she raised a visibly trembling hand to cover lips that even now craved the touch of his. Seeing it, his own mouth curved into a tight line and a muscle started to tick in his jaw.

'Don't worry, Kate, you'll remain inviolate. That was only a sample of what I would do if you break the rules. You see, I have my conditions too. I'll agree to your terms so long as you obey mine. There will be none of your usual tricks while you remain married to me. Other men are out, as of now. Play the part of my devoted wife, and you'll remain as virginal as the day you were born. But try to play with me, or anyone else, and the contract is void. Is that understood?'

Kate had difficulty concentrating. Her eyes followed the movement of his lips like a magnet, though her ears scarcely heard the words. They seemed to come from a long way away. When at last they penetrated her consciousness, she flinched. Swallowing hard, she had never been so thankful to have her reaction misinterpreted. What had seemed like aeons to her had been no time at all. He had no idea of her startling reaction to his touch. And he never would. She wasn't fool enough to place in his hands any weapon that he could use against her. Right now, he thought that, wanting no man's touch on the purity of her body, she feared him. She was only too happy to let him carry on thinking that way, for the truth was much more potentially devastating.

'Yes, I understand,' she croaked. Her throat dry and aching, she went on in a strained voice, 'Now you understand this. Don't you ever, *ever* touch me again!'

The implied threat bounced off him. 'Don't give me cause to,' he returned smoothly. 'So, we have a deal?'

Every protective instinct screamed at her to say no, but she had given her word. 'Yes.' That one word rang with the slamming of any escape route.

His smile failed to reach his eyes. 'Good. I'm glad we understand each other.' With a carelessly graceful movement, he shot back his cuff and glanced at his watch. 'It's late. I'll leave now, but we still have a great deal to discuss. I'll pick you up at one tomorrow, and we'll talk over lunch.' He was already moving towards the door as he spoke.

Kate walked with him like an automaton. He left with a mocking rejoinder to sleep well. Severely provoked, she only just managed to stop herself from slamming the door behind him.

Sleep well! She doubted that she would ever sleep soundly again after tonight. Sagging back against the closed door, Kate raised her fingers to her lips wonderingly. She could still feel the touch of his, burning her hotly, and she moaned faintly. How had it happened? One moment he had been an angry antagonist, the next he had turned her world upside-down. She, Kate, who hadn't thought she could feel anything, had been aroused to her very core by Aidan Crawford of all people!

Why him? The question taunted her. He despised her. He certainly hadn't forgiven her, and felt no respect for her at all. To come alive at one kiss from him wasn't a fairy-tale, it was madness. Sheer lunacy that must not happen again. She had got away with it because he hadn't expected her to respond, but she couldn't always count on being that fortunate.

In future, her defences must be rock-solid, until she had this unfortunate attraction under control. It surely wouldn't be long. Good heavens, she didn't even like the man! No, it was just one of those crazy things that would pass, and until it did she would just have to be on her mettle. In that he was on her side.

He thought she was a virgin who was determined to remain one because no man was good enough to touch her. It was a lie she was going to have to uphold because she certainly wouldn't tell him that until he'd kissed her she had believed herself to be frigid, unable to respond physically to a man. Yet, in perpetuating the lie, she would have to perpetuate the character she had just come to realise she didn't want to be. It was a cruel irony that she wasn't going to be allowed to change on the outside, when on the inside she was already a different person. She knew she could play the Ice Queen standing on her head, but the trouble was that it would no longer be any real protection. She was vulnerable inside to hurts that the old Kate hadn't been aware of.

She knew now she had agreed to walk a path fraught with danger. Just how she was going to survive the journey lay in the lap of the gods.

CHAPTER FIVE

As soon as Kate reached her office the next morning she sent for Rae. Her assistant arrived full of her usual good humour, making Kate, who had hardly slept a wink, feel even more hung over. There had been an added refinement to her bad dream last night. Far from being an isolated incident, it had intensified. It had begun to take shape and form. No longer shadows, yet not quite substance. She had never felt so threatened before, and it had showed in the pale face and haunted eyes that confronted her in her mirror. Only excellent make-up had helped to hide the worst of the ravages.

She was tired and overwrought, and not up to what she had to do today. Removing the slim jacket that matched her black pencil skirt, which today she had teamed with a violet silk blouse, she sat down at her desk and took a deep breath.

'How would you feel about holding the fort for me for the next few weeks, Rae?' she asked without preamble.

Her friend's eyes widened. 'Why? Where will you be?'

Kate's nails tapped out a nervy tattoo on the desk-top. 'I'll be on honeymoon. I'm getting married.'

'Married!' Rae sat down with a thump on the nearest chair. 'Did you say married?' she queried faintly, as if doubting her sanity—or Kate's—or both.

'I did,' Kate nodded, watching Rae's disbelief turn to concern. 'Do you think you'll cope?' she added quickly, hoping to avert the uncomfortable questions she saw forming.

Rae waved a hand irritably. 'Of course, once I get over the shock. But this is all very sudden. If it isn't a secret, would you care to tell me who the prospective bridegroom is? Not Jonathan?' she queried in some alarm.

Kate pulled a face, but was glad of the momentary reprieve. 'No, not Jonathan. In fact, we won't be seeing each other again. His decision, not mine.'

Rae gave a silent whistle. 'Chucked you, did he? I didn't think he had it in him.'

'Neither did I.' Kate recalled her own astonishment wryly.

'So, who is it, then?' Rae persisted.

This was the moment Kate had been dreading, but there was no avoiding it. 'Aidan Crawford,' she supplied levelly.

The way Rae's chin dropped would have been funny if Kate had been in the mood for laughing. 'Oh, my God, Kate! What on earth are you doing?'

'It's a long and complicated story——'

'Just the sort I like,' Rae interrupted swiftly. 'I'm sitting comfortably, so you'd better begin.'

With a helpless sigh, Kate bowed to the inevitable. As concisely as possible she related the essence of her meetings with the Crawfords. Rae listened silently, a deep frown creasing her forehead as Kate came to the end.

'It's all very well to be noble, Kate, but marriage?'

'There's no other way,' Kate said quietly. 'Besides, I gave my word.'

Rae sighed helplessly, knowing only too well the significance of that. 'I hope you know what you're doing. OK, I know it's supposed to be a business arrangement, but what do you know of him, really? Did you know he's thought to be the sexiest man this side of the Pond? They say he's got what it takes by the bushel.'

Recalling her own reaction to him, Kate's colour rose as she was unable to deny it.

Rae hadn't finished yet. 'Someone at the party recognised him. They were only too keen to pass on that information. The betting as to whether he would succeed where others had failed was quite brisk,' she concluded bluntly.

Kate flinched. 'Oh.'

Rae instantly reached out a hand. 'Me and my big mouth! But you hurt a lot of people, Kate, and the business you're in isn't the kindest. The best thing you can do is forget it. That's all in the past now, anyway. The point is, I have a bad feeling about this.'

This was no time for Kate to admit that she felt the same. She had to be confident. 'I'll be all right. I'm not his type. And as you well know, I'm not about to put myself into a dangerous situation. I *have* to do this, Rae. I really don't think I have any choice.' She fell silent, feeling that sense of fatalism quite distinctly. A dull headache had started up, and she rubbed at it, trying to ease it.

Rae watched her thoughtfully. 'Headache?'

Kate sighed. 'I didn't sleep too well.'

'It's more than that. I know the signs, Kate. You look drawn. What's wrong?'

Unable to repress a shiver, Kate looked up. 'It's nothing, really, just some bad dreams. A reaction to stress. Everyone has them,' she insisted, as if trying to convince herself rather than her friend.

'Does everyone look like you do after them? Do you want to talk about it?' Rae offered. 'Doesn't it seem a bit odd to you that you should get them now? Perhaps something triggered it off? The only thing that's happened lately is Aidan Crawford's eruption on to the scene. Could there be a connection?'

Kate's nerves rioted. 'Of course, but it would only be due to stress. A guilty conscience at work. So please can we forget it?' she begged, wanting the distressing conversation to end. It was bad enough having the dreams without dissecting them too. 'What I really wanted to know was if you'd be a witness.'

Rae seemed about to protest the change of subject, then let it pass with a defeated shrug of her shoulders. 'I'd never speak to you again if you hadn't asked me. We've been through a lot together, and I won't desert you now. Even if I think you are crazy,' she added drily.

Later, when Rae had gone, Kate sagged with relief. That was one hurdle over. The most difficult was yet to come. With a sigh she reached for a folder of letters and buried herself in work. There was a great deal to be done, loose ends tidied up, before she could leave the running of the agency in Rae's capable hands. It would mean that for a while, at least, she wouldn't have to think.

At five to one, Rae popped her head around the door, her expression bland. 'There's a Mr Crawford to see you.'

Over at the filing cabinet, the nerves in Kate's stomach lurched and twisted themselves into a knot. 'Thank you, Rae,' she returned levelly, and would have asked for a few minutes to compose herself, only her assistant stepped neatly aside to allow Aidan Crawford into the room.

She had thought she was prepared to meet him, had regained her control after last night's startling revelation. But the second he walked into the room, she knew she was wrong. Even as her heart started a crazy beat, she was telling herself he was just a man, and she knew how to handle them. Stay cool and distant, that was all it would take. But it didn't work out that way.

Hands closing on the cold metal of the drawer, her knowledgeable eye took in the fact that the grey suit he wore today was by Armani, no less. It fitted his long-

legged, leanly muscular physique to perfection, and she
was suddenly tossed into the stormy seas of her newly
awakened senses.

She had never experienced anything like it. The impact
was electric, as if someone had plugged the room into
the mains. Her skin prickled. It seemed as if every inch
of her was aware of every inch of him. Such intense
physical attraction was uncharted territory for Kate. It
frightened even as it exhilarated. She knew that, even if
the room had been crowded, her sensitised radar would
have picked up his presence. It was uncanny, as if she
had been programmed to respond to just this one man.
She recalled that kiss vividly, and her lips tingled. Deep
inside her, something throbbed into life.

Unable to move, she couldn't take her eyes off him.
In thrall, she knew how it felt to be a rabbit caught by
the headlights of a car.

A sardonic smile hovered about his mouth as he
crossed the room towards her, purpose in every stride.
Dulled as her reactions were, she realised what he
intended to do and weakly put out a hand to ward him
off. It proved to be a fatal mistake, for he captured her
hand neatly and used it to pull her towards him so that
he could press on her lips the kiss she had wanted to
avoid.

Her reaction was instantaneous. She went up like dry
tinder. She seemed to have no bones, and her blood
turned thick and hot in her veins. Heavy eyelids closed
over dazed eyes. Helplessly her lips parted at the touch
of his, their sensitive skin aching to respond, only there
was no time. The merest brush of his lips over hers, and
then he was lifting his head again, leaving her blinking
bewilderedly up at him.

'Darling,' he greeted smoothly. Kate's colour fluctuated wildly. She heard Rae's sharp intake of breath
before she shut the door on them.

She was set free immediately. He moved away from her, back rigid with rejection, leaving her in no doubt, should she have wondered, that his actions were purely for show. While she had been overwhelmed by the sensations going through her. Dear God, he only had to touch her and she was like putty in his hands! It had been last night all over again, only much more intense. She could hardly credit her own complete loss of self.

But at least he hadn't guessed. Though she had done nothing to help herself, her secret was still safe. Hating herself for feeling an attraction that was so one-sided, she slammed the file drawer closed with a clatter.

'Why did you do that?' she demanded angrily, not a little of that anger directed at herself. How close she had come to betraying herself!

Resting on a corner of her desk, he studied her curiously. A strange light glittered in his eyes. 'Just setting the scene,' he murmured drily.

A shiver ran down her spine as she saw that light. He couldn't have guessed. There hadn't been time. She looked at him, swallowing hard, but whatever she had thought she had seen was gone. She crossed her arms. 'Well, you don't have to bother for Rae's benefit. She knows exactly why I'm marrying you. So I'd rather you kept your hands to yourself. I don't want to be touched, and I certainly don't want to be kissed!' Liar! her senses accused. Her body was so vitally aware of him that her breasts actually ached. Like a schoolgirl with a crush, she wanted more, not less. It was like a fever! Kate stiffened her spine. Everyone knew how hotly a fever burned, but, if you starved it, it would die down. That was what she had to do. She was crazy to feel anything for this man, and it would be insanity to allow him to find out that she did!

He looked grimly amused. 'I know that well enough without your telling me,' he declared harshly. 'The way you freeze off a man speaks for itself. But brace yourself, my sweet Kate. Perhaps your friend didn't expect me to kiss you, but plenty of other people will. *We* know this marriage is a business deal, but everyone else has to believe it's real. To do that we'll have to hide our mutual aversion and pretend we love each other. For that, I'll kiss you when and where I have to, and I'll expect you to respond.'

Kate was glad her hands were hidden because the way they started to tremble would have been telling. The pictures he conjured up sent flames licking her skin. She felt like a punch-drunk boxer. After years of celibacy, suddenly one man had kissed her twice and she was experiencing the heady sweet tug of desire. So far she had been able to hide it from him, but if he carried out his threat she didn't know how long she could keep on doing so.

She called herself all sorts of a fool for not considering all their agreement would entail. He'd expect them to kiss and touch as normal lovers would. And because she was bound by her word, there was no way out of it. A shudder ran through her at the idea. But once again it wasn't quite fear.

He saw the betraying movement and misread it. Anger sparkled in his grey eyes. 'Come down off that pedestal you're so proud of, Kate, or I'll force you down. My touch won't contaminate you. Remember, a shower will quickly restore you to that state of unsullied virtue you admire in yourself,' he reminded her contemptuously. 'Tell me, doesn't it ever get lonely up there in that rarefied atmosphere?'

Kate drew in a very painful breath. Never had she had to face such withering scorn, and with little or no armour to fight it. At all costs she had to bolster his misconception. 'You're enjoying this, aren't you?' she challenged huskily.

He stood abruptly and moved to the window, his back to her. 'It has a novelty value I hadn't looked for. I don't think I'm going to be bored,' he agreed mockingly, and turned, hands braced behind him on the sill. 'You don't like male men, do you, Kate? You like to be the dominant one. Unfortunately for you, this marriage will have only one master—me. It should prove quite instructive for you—and entertaining for me.'

'I won't be used as any man's entertainment, Mr Crawford!' she declared thickly, welcoming the anger she felt at his statement. 'I'm a human being, not an object you can pick up and put down as you please!'

Grey eyes glittered triumphantly as he said softly, 'Neither am I, Kate. Nor were any of the men you discarded so blithely.'

Trumped, Kate could only stare back at him impotently, knowing it was true. Her heart took up a sickening thud.

'Look on it as poetic justice,' he went on when she remained silent, 'and take your medicine like a good little girl. To start with, my name is Aidan. You'd better get used to saying it, because nobody is going to believe in a marriage where you go around calling your husband Mr Crawford.'

He had her backed into a corner, and the only way to hide her inner turmoil was to come out fighting.

'It would serve you right if I called the whole thing off. Then what would you do—with no wife?' The jeer was pure Ice Queen.

Aidan's nostrils flared as he took an angry breath. 'I'd do the best I could on my own.'

'And lose!'

His eyes narrowed. 'Probably. But you won't call it off, will you, Kate? Not if you want me to believe you possess a heart after all. You're doing this for me, aren't

you? Or was I right when I said it was still revenge you
wanted?'

Once again he held the trump card, and Kate had to
swallow her anger with an effort. 'Damn you!'

He laughed at her chagrin. 'You'd better get your act
together, my love. Now, if you're ready, we'll go. I've
a table booked for one-thirty.'

Without another word she turned her back on him,
reaching for her jacket. But before she could put it on
he had taken it from her and was holding it out for her
to slip her arms in. He met her startled blue gaze with
a raised eyebrow, and there was nothing for Kate to do
but accept his assistance. The possessive weight of his
hands on her shoulders was a silent reminder of his
dominance. She stood still because her pride wouldn't
let her run, but she had to close her eyes, and suddenly
she felt as if she were in a long dark tunnel, aware only
of possessive hands on her shoulders—but not the same
hands at all. She gasped, and instantly the feeling was
gone, leaving behind only the shuddering reaction of a
nightmare.

Shaken to the core, she felt herself pale as the tremor
ran through her. Dear lord, what was happening to her?
Was she going mad? The thought tumbled round and
round her brain, so it was some seconds before she
became aware that Aidan's hands still held her.

He had to have felt her shock, and she knew he had
when he turned her round. She refused to look at him,
but he countered that by tipping her chin with a firm
hand. She saw the shock in his face as for a brief moment
he saw what she had striven to keep hidden—the fear
and distress in her eyes. It caused his grip to slacken and
she pulled away then, dipping her head and compressing
her lips.

'Kate?' Her name was an appalled question she
ignored and she grabbed up her purse from the desk.

She had never experienced anything like that before, and why had he had to be there to witness it? Whatever it was, she didn't want to talk about it. Didn't even want to think of it! When she turned to face him, she was in control once more.

'Let's go, shall we?' she said in clipped tones, and didn't wait for an answer but swept out of the door. With a muffled imprecation, she heard him follow her.

He didn't attempt to stop her until they were outside in the street, but once there, he caught her by the arm and swung her round.

'What happened in there?'

Kate widened her eyes. 'Happened?'

A nerve ticked in his jaw. 'You know damn well what I mean, Kate. For a moment you looked—afraid, and it's not the first time it's happened either.'

'Don't be ridiculous,' she scoffed with a tight little laugh, alarmed at his perception. 'How could *I* possibly be afraid?'

'Exactly what I thought, and yet I know what I saw.'

From the determination in his eyes, she knew he wasn't about to drop the subject, and it occurred to her that the best form of defence was attack. With a practised ease, she cast a provocative look up at him through her lashes.

'Did you feel sorry for me, Aidan?' At her question, she had the doubtful felicity of seeing his expression wiped clean.

'I see.' The two words chased chills up her spine. 'I thought I'd warned you against playing off your tricks on me, Kate.'

She had never realised quite how threatening a soft voice could be. But, having set her course, she wasn't about to change tack. What had happened was private. Almost a waking nightmare. Perhaps it *was* part of her nightmares, and they were things she could never discuss with anyone, let alone him. So, she brazened it out. 'You did, but I had to see if you really meant it.'

'Now you know I did. And now I know what you're capable of, I won't be falling for that line again. Now let's get the hell away from here before I'm tempted to throttle the lying breath out of you!' he gritted through his teeth, and set off down the street at a pace she had to trot to keep up with.

Aidan had booked a table in one of those French restaurants so often found tucked away in side-streets. They were shown to a secluded corner where they could talk without fear of being overheard. He ordered for both of them without consulting her, and Kate, her appetite completely vanished, would have argued if she hadn't seen the challenging glint in his eye and decided not to rise to the bait. It was galling, though, to see his lips curve in amusement at her caution.

Sipping at a glass of white wine while they waited for their meal to arrive, Kate broke the silence that was making her feel distinctly edgy, even though she had sworn not to speak first. 'So, what happens now?'

Across the table, Aidan casually crossed his legs. A movement that drew her eyes and dried her mouth at the way the material stretched over his muscular thighs. He was as graceful as a big cat, and just as dangerous, as he relaxed back in his seat, clearly enjoying having her at a disadvantage. 'I'll arrange a special licence. We can be married by the end of the week.'

Though she had been expecting something like this, her stomach still knotted anxiously. 'So soon?' Good lord, did her voice have to sound so croaky!

Aidan regarded her steadily. 'We have no time to lose. My birthday is only days away. There's no time for a formal wedding, and the fewer people who know about this, the better,' he finished grimly.

'You mean . . . your brother?'

'I mean that the Press would have a field day if they got wind of the fact that, days after I should have married one woman, I marry the woman who stopped that marriage by claiming she was my wife. That kind of publicity I can do without. So far I've managed to keep last Saturday's fiasco out of the papers.'

Kate chewed on her lip. 'Would it prejudice your case?' That particular angle hadn't occurred to her, and now that it did it brought with it another wave of guilt.

'Frankly, I doubt it. A marriage is all the will requires. But I'd rather not have to put it to the test. My grandfather's eccentricities could have further codicils as yet undisclosed. I presume I *can* trust you not to talk?'

That brought a spark to her eye. 'Would you accept my word if I gave it?'

For answer he rested both arms on the table and leant forward. 'There's an old Arab proverb which says, "Trust in Allah, but tie up your camel." On your recent behaviour, can you give me one good reason why I should trust you?'

That was one goad too many. 'Because you don't have a choice?' She smiled at him sweetly.

It was probably fortunate that the waiter arrived with their meal at that point, because Aidan's face had darkened dramatically. He was forced to hold his tongue, however, and Kate jumped in quickly as the waiter departed, deflecting what he might have said.

'If your grandfather entrusted the company to you, why did he make that will?' she asked curiously.

Aidan's laugh was soft. 'Because he didn't approve of my lifestyle. Like any other young man, I played the field. That was acceptable so far as it went, but the old man expected me to settle down one day. Unfortunately, marriage never appealed to me after I'd seen the results of my own parents' marriage, and divorce. We didn't see eye to eye, and I could be as stubborn as he. But the old goat won in the end, didn't he? If I wanted control of the company, I had to find a good woman to marry and, more importantly, become the mother of my sons.'

To Kate he didn't sound bitter at all, more wryly affectionate. Whatever their differences, they had respected each other. She wished she could have been privy to some of their battles. They would have been very illuminating!

'And now that's me,' she said softly, feeling a strange curling warmth inside her.

'God forbid!'

Hurt seemed to explode inside her, touching every nerve at the same moment, so that no part of her was free of it. 'You don't think I have what it takes to be a good mother?' By some miracle the words came out coolly.

He eyed her soberly for so long that she felt ready to squirm in her seat before he replied. 'For us the question is irrelevant, but as a matter of fact I do. I've seen you with children. You can't hide that sort of affection.'

Crazily, Kate felt again that warm glow of pleasure at his words, and it left her feeling confused. 'Thanks,' she said gruffly. A thought occurred to her. 'Would you have remained married to Julia?'

'That was the general idea. However, you can rest assured, Kate, that our marriage will be strictly temporary.'

Instead of being reassured, Kate experienced a stab of pure jealousy. It left her confused and irritated, and that was reflected in her sharp tone as she said, 'Won't it look strange if you turn up with a completely different woman as your wife?'

Aidan shook his head. 'Fortunately no. Stateside, only my father and Netta, my stepmother, knew I was getting married.'

Kate frowned heavily. 'But surely they'll find it odd?'

Again he shook his head, and there was a curve of grim amusement about his mouth. 'They were at the wedding so they know I'm not marrying Julia. They flew home yesterday before I heard from you, but I rang them later. They know all about you.'

The room seemed to tilt alarmingly. 'All? You can't mean...?'

'Oh, but I do. They know you were the mystery woman, and they know you've agreed to help me out. They're willing to accept you on those terms.'

She stared at him, appalled. 'How could you? My God, they must despise me!'

'For that you've only yourself to blame. If you want respect, you have to earn it,' he shot back with both barrels.

Kate reeled as blow followed blow. 'I think I hate you!' she said through gritted teeth.

Aidan uttered a harsh laugh and leant across the table towards her. 'Do you, Kate? Well, to mangle a quote, I don't give a damn. All that matters is that we give a convincing performance while we're in the States.'

'The States?' Kate gasped, 'But I thought...'

He smiled tightly. 'We'd have a honeymoon?' he finished for her.

'Well...yes.' He'd said he was having one with Julia, so naturally she'd assumed...

He followed her thoughts. 'Julia and I would have had two weeks. It was all I could afford due to business commitments. So I'm afraid you'll just have to do without a honeymoon, Kate. My father lives in Washington; we'll be flying over to stay with him after the wedding. So that means no more Ice Queen, Kate. Winter's over, it's time to thaw. Make up your mind to it. As soon as we touch down in America, the curtain goes up on our little play, and I'm expecting nothing less than rave reviews on your performance.'

CHAPTER SIX

KATE stared out into the darkness, oblivious of her slim figure reflected in the window of the hotel room. In the light she could see the snow falling. Winter in New York. How romantic it sounded. Perhaps for others it was, but not for her. Sighing, she let the heavy brocade curtain drop back into place, blocking out the cold, and glanced at her watch. It was nearly six o'clock. Very soon now, Aidan was going to return. The thought simply made her feel colder.

The past week had been hectic, punctuated by the recurring bad dreams. The effect was noticeable. She had lost weight she could ill afford, her appetite dwindling to nothing. Thankfully there had been no repeat of that incident in her office, and she had managed to rationalise it away as just a freakish isolated occurrence.

It hadn't been so easy to come to terms with her unwanted attraction for her husband. She had seen him only briefly before the wedding, and on those occasions she had been too keenly aware of him, though he hadn't as much as touched her. Mostly he had kept in contact by telephone, but even his voice had the ability to raise the fine hairs all over her body. It had become an act of total concentration not to give away the smallest sign of what she was undergoing, and it was exhausting.

Aidan's mood had been difficult to calculate. Their meetings had been businesslike to the point of abruptness. He would arrive, give her his instructions and then leave as soon as possible, which had hardly been a boost to her confidence.

They had been married only that morning in the presence of Rae and a man whose name she couldn't call to mind—Tim somebody or other. To prove it she wore the rings Aidan had given her on her marriage finger. She had protested about the engagement ring, but he had bought it for her anyway, and now it sat, a round sapphire surrounded by diamonds, next to the chased gold band. An uncompromising symbol of the fact that she was now his wife.

The die had been well and truly cast.

There had been no celebration; there hadn't been time. They had gone straight to the airport to catch their flight to New York. Not Washington, as she had expected. She had found out why when they'd arrived here at their hotel. No sooner had the porter left than Aidan had gathered up his briefcase, informed her he had a business meeting, and disappeared. She had been alone ever since.

Alone she had discovered that their suite consisted of two rooms, a sitting-room and a twin-bedded bedroom with en-suite bathroom. Foolishly, it had never occurred to her that they would have to share the same bedroom. As far as she could see, there was absolutely no reason why they should, and every reason why they shouldn't. Sharing a room, there were a hundred ways she could give herself away. Besides, the chances were high that she would have those dreams again. They were getting worse, scarcely missing a night. She absolutely didn't want him to witness that. It would be the final humiliation. When he came back, she was going to demand that he find them alternative accommodation.

Almost as if she had magicked him, Aidan walked through the door. Tossing his briefcase on to a chair, he tugged at the knot of his tie. Kate thought he looked tired, but right now that wasn't as important as her own problem. Already tense at the idea of this confrontation as she was, her tingling reaction to his appearance only added to the strain.

'Have you any idea what time it is? Where have you been?' she demanded crossly.

He looked at her, eyebrows mockingly raised. 'How very wifely you sound, Kate. Does that mean you missed me?'

'Do I look as though I've suddenly gone mad?' she shot back scornfully.

To her surprise, he laughed, a deep, warm sound that chased shivers up her spine. 'Admittedly not. But you do look as though someone's ruffled your feathers. Are you going to tell me what's wrong, or do I have to guess?' he enquired sardonically, moving across to the drinks cabinet and pouring himself a straight Scotch.

Kate held her temper by a whisker, having learned by now when he was being deliberately provocative. It had been this way all week. Almost as if he was testing her to see how far he could push her before she exploded. Well, she hadn't, and wouldn't, give him that satisfaction.

'I want to change this suite,' she told him shortly.

That irritating eyebrow rose again. 'Demands so soon? Don't tell me, the colour doesn't match your beautiful blue eyes.'

He very nearly knocked her off balance with that. Beautiful eyes! She hadn't thought he would find any-thing about her beautiful. Startled by her own thoughts, she stared at him, and only belatedly saw his watchful amusement and realised she had been neatly diverted.

'Don't patronise me, Aidan. You know what I mean. I want a bedroom of my own.'

He took a sip from his glass before saying simply, 'No.'

Her lips parted on a tiny gasp. 'What do you mean, no?'

Aidan settled himself on the couch and stretched out his legs. 'Are you having difficulty with the language? No means no. Or let me put it another way. Short though this marriage might be, I intend to start as I mean to go on. I'm not putting its credibility in doubt by having separate bedrooms.'

Kate crossed her arms to hide the sudden tremor of her hands. 'And my feelings don't count, I suppose?' she demanded huskily.

'They're a luxury I can't afford. Count your blessings that you have a bed to yourself. As for bedrooms, one is all we need,' Aidan informed her bluntly and tossed off the remains of his Scotch.

'Then I'll sleep in here. I take it you have no objections if I sleep on the couch?' Kate snapped sarcastically, wishing for the hundredth time that she had thought of this before agreeing to marry him.

His grey eyes narrowed on her thoughtfully. 'What's the matter, Kate?' he asked softly. 'Afraid you'll reveal more secrets?'

Every nerve in her body seemed to jolt violently. Her legs felt suddenly too weak to hold her, and she sank down rather hurriedly on the arm of the couch. 'Secrets? I don't know what you mean.' Oh, lord, what now?

Aidan looked at her keenly, then, setting his glass aside, he put his hands behind his head. 'Don't you know you talk in your sleep?' he asked curiously.

For a moment, she really thought she was going to faint. Her heart started to race, and yet it felt as if it was being squeezed in a vice. She paled. 'What?'

'I said, don't you know you talk in your sleep?' he obligingly repeated. 'You were quite eloquent on the flight over.'

Talk in her sleep? She couldn't have—could she? She had been tired enough to sleep. Could she have spoken aloud? If so, what had she said? Panic was only a step away, and she fought it down with anger. 'Is this some perverted sort of joke? I assure you I don't find it funny.'

'No, I can see that,' he mused. 'I wonder why. What are you afraid of?'

Oh, God! Her chin came up. 'Nothing! And I *don't* talk in my sleep,' Kate insisted firmly.

Aidan's smile was bland. 'How would you know? You were asleep at the time.'

If he wanted her rattled, then she was, seriously. But he was the last person who would know it. She rallied, forcing herself to remain calm. Her shrug was a master-piece of acting. 'Interesting, was it? I'd *hate* to think I was boring you.' She sounded bored, whereas she was desperate to know what she had said—even as she dreaded that knowledge.

'Interesting? It probably was. I couldn't say,' Aidan parried aggravatingly.

God, how he was enjoying watching her squirm, the rat! 'Why not?' she demanded angrily, watching the smile cross his face. 'Oh, I get it! You intend to hold it over my head, is that it?'

His teeth flashed whitely. 'What a suspicious mind you have, Kate Crawford. Could you really reveal anything dreadful enough for blackmail?'

This time she didn't attempt to shrug it off. 'I don't know. You tell me,' she gritted out between her teeth.

A laugh rumbled up from way down in his chest. 'Now that sounds like a very guilty conscience talking. My, my, Kate, what have you been up to?'

She knew then, knew she hadn't said anything at all. He had just wound her up and she, fool that she was, had walked straight into it. 'Damn you! It was just a big try on, wasn't it?'

'And you fell for it. Never mind, Kate. Call it one for the boys. Besides, it wasn't a total lie, although mumble would be a better description than talk.'

Kate stared at him for a moment, then took a deep breath. 'This is the way it's going to be, is it? I have to pretend to be happily married, while you take cheap shots? I don't think that's going to fool anybody.'

Aidan sobered and slowly sat up to rub a hand around his neck. 'You're right, it won't,' he admitted, then he grinned reminiscently. 'But you rose so beautifully that I couldn't resist it.'

Kate stared at him, a slow anger coming to the boil like a pot on a stove. While she had been worried to death, he had been teasing!

'Why, you...!' She looked around for something to throw, found only the cushion, and launched herself at him, using it like a weapon.

After his first stunned reaction, Aidan sprang into action, fielding the swings neatly until he could make a grab for the cushion. All the while a slow rumble of laughter came from him.

'My, my, Kate, this isn't very regal of you!' he gasped, dodging as she flailed away.

Liking the sound of his laughter, but hating him, Kate growled and swung harder—only to miss him completely. With a yelp she spun round, losing her balance. But she didn't fall, for an arm snaked round her hips, fielding her neatly, and in the next instant she was lying on the couch, breathing heavily, with Aidan's long body stretched over hers, his arms about her—a gleam in his eye that twisted her heart.

Their eyes locked, and everything seemed to go still. In breathless fascination she watched the colour in his eyes deepen. Saw the way his gaze dropped to her lips. They tingled as if he had already touched them, and a tiny moan escaped her. His head rose, cheeks flushed, and she saw the moment when he thought of drawing back overthrown by a compulsion that was too strong.

'Kate.' His voice was a husky groan as he lowered his head to hers.

If he had kept silent, she might have kept her head, but the passion in his voice was her undoing. His lips moved hungrily on hers, tasting, biting, seeking a response that, with a whimper of need, she gave willingly. Her lips parted, welcoming his invasion, and the world burst into flames around her. It was as if the battle went on, yet now their arms clung, hands offering fevered caresses that raised body heat to scorching point.

What Kate had felt when she alone responded was as nothing to this. She ached to be touched, to touch. Gloried in the arousal of his body grinding against hers. Every kiss sought to quench this dizzying spiral of need, but only added fuel to a fire that rapidly threatened to blaze out of all control.

His mouth left hers, searing a path down her neck that brought tiny gasps of pleasure to her lips. Nimbly his hands dealt with the buttons of her jacket, pushing it aside to reveal the swollen perfection of her breasts in their thin lace covering. Slowly one hand glided up to possess one peak, and it felt to Kate as if he had claimed her very soul. She cried out and Aidan went still, raising eyes gleaming hot with passion.

'Sweet heaven, Kate, but I want you,' he growled huskily, voice tinged with shock.

It was that which brought sanity back with a vengeance, crashing her down to earth, to shiver in the aftermath. What was she doing? He wanted her, but he hadn't expected to, probably didn't even really want to. Yet he'd take her because she had just shown she was willing—very, very willing. But afterwards, what then? He didn't love her or need her. She was a convenience, no more. While he was used to a casual fling, she wasn't, and never would be. But even more importantly she had been criminally careless, forgetting how serious a risk she would have been taking.

Thanking whatever gods prevailed for bringing her to her senses in time, she pushed him away and clambered hastily to her feet. Still shaking, she kept her back to him.

'That wasn't part of the deal, remember?' she declared icily, fastening buttons haphazardly.

She heard the brush of cloth as he stood up, then he was swinging her round to face him, anger stamped all over him. 'What the hell does that mean?'

Kate lifted her chin. 'Just a reminder to keep your hands to yourself in future.'

'You wanted me,' he ground out thickly.

'And then I didn't,' she returned, acid-sweet, hating herself for the way his face closed over.

His eyes flashed a warning. 'Why, you little...!' he bit off harshly. 'I see, still playing your tricks, are you, Your Highness? There's a word for women like you—but I guess you've heard that already,' he added scornfully. 'Just so far and no further, eh, Kate? That's a dangerous tactic. You can push a man too far by heating him up and then freezing him off. But don't worry, I'll keep my lustful hands to myself in future!'

Feeling flayed to the bone, she forced herself not to look away. 'Good!' she snapped back.

Aidan shook his head. 'Lady, you are something else! It's a good thing we're going out, otherwise I might be tempted to throttle the life out of you.'

Nerves jolting, she ignored the threat. 'Going out?' she queried, mouth drying as she watched him refasten shirt buttons she must have undone only minutes ago.

'The man I saw today has invited us to join him and his wife for dinner. When he heard we hadn't had a celebration, he booked a table at one of the top nightspots.'

'Why didn't you stop him?' she exclaimed at once.

He ran a tired hand through his hair. 'Because we have to start somewhere. If we have any rough spots, I want them ironed out.'

Loath as she was to admit it, he had a point. She had never had much confidence about fooling people. At least this way they would have a trial run. Even so, there could be problems.

'Do they know about Julia?' she asked anxiously.

'No. Mitch is a business colleague. I dine with him and his wife Sarah when I'm in New York. So you won't be expected to know things from my past. Any ignorance we do show will have a good excuse. It was a whirlwind romance, remember. We have the rest of our lives to get to know each other.' There was more than a hint of mockery in his tone as he finished, and his eyes gleamed at her.

This time she didn't rise. 'Thank heavens for small mercies! A little knowledge of you goes a long way. Like paraffin. You spill a small drop, and everything for miles around smells, tastes and oozes it!'

His eyes followed her as she gracefully crossed the room to the bedroom door. 'Do I detect a note of criticism?'

'I wouldn't have the nerve,' she rejoined shortly.

'Sweetheart, you've got nerve enough for anything—I know.'

It seemed a good note to leave on, and Kate went through the door. In the bedroom, she leant back against the door and eyed the two large beds. That had been a very narrow escape, but the Ice Queen had saved her once again. She winced at the memory of his scorn. She hadn't meant to tease, but it would have been madness to give in to an attraction that had no future. She closed her eyes. How her body ached with the promise of fulfilment denied. She'd have to be more careful. If he should ever guess how vulnerable she really was, how false the Ice Queen was, what would he do? If he really tried to seduce her she knew she'd have no weapons to fight him. She'd surrender before the first shot was even fired! She couldn't afford that.

She looked at the beds again. It wasn't going to be easy, sharing this room. Though she had stated her intention of sleeping on the couch, she knew realistically that she couldn't. That option wouldn't be open to her at his parents' home. She would have to get used to sharing, and tonight was all she had. The thought knotted her stomach. Aidan might believe she had the nerve to do anything, but this was something else entirely.

She hadn't bothered to unpack just for one night. Now she retrieved an uncrushable violet jersey dress from her case, together with fresh underwear, and took them into the bathroom. There was a lock on the door and she used it, knowing that Aidan would have no qualms about walking in if she didn't.

Wrapping a towel around her hair to keep it dry, she showered swiftly, dried herself on a luxuriously thick bath sheet, then stepped into the chocolate silk and lace teddy. Make-up came next, and her years as a model had got its application down to a fine art, so that it hardly looked as if she was wearing any at all. Lastly came the dress. It was soft and clingy, with long sleeves and a cowl neckline. It was a particular favourite, and she generally wore it when her confidence needed a boost. Tonight seemed to fit the bill perfectly.

Satisfied at last with her appearance, Kate gathered up her discarded clothes. The white suit that she had been married in looked tired and forlorn draped over her arm. Reflecting some of her own feelings. Banishing the maudlin thought, she unlocked the door and re-entered the bedroom, only to be brought up short by the sight of her husband standing mere yards away, clad only in his trousers.

During her career, Kate had become inured to the sight of near-naked males. She had classed them in her mind as models, and therefore sexless. The same couldn't be said about Aidan. His chest was broad and tanned, well-developed and with a fine mat of silky dark hair.

Staring, transfixed, she went hot and cold. Memory of those heated moments in his arms stirred her body into vibrant life. Dear God, he was so tall, so broad and strong. Fully clad, he was a force to be reckoned with. Now, barely clothed, he looked like some lethal, proud jungle animal. Intensely male. Her throat closed over and her mouth went dry. The pull to go across and run her hands over his taut skin was so strong, she had taken a step before she even knew it. Appalled at her wanton thoughts, she took her anger out on him.

'Must you do that here?' Even to her own ears her voice was high-pitched and tense, and she couldn't look him in the eye. She flung the clothes down and rummaged in her case for her black shoes and black leather belt with hands that shook.

Aidan, meanwhile, had looked up in surprise from unfastening the buttons of a clean shirt. 'Do what?'

Her fingers trembled so badly, it took two attempts to fasten the belt in the right hole. 'Change,' she snapped.

Aidan dropped the shirt into the case. 'Oh? And just where would you have me do it? In the corridor?'

Her feet went into her shoes in two jerky movements. 'There is a bathroom.'

'Which you were using until thirty seconds ago,' he pointed out. 'Even so, I'm not standing here naked, Kate, so I'm at a loss to understand this show of outraged modesty.'

Kate looked up, ready to shoot back an answer, but lost the ability to utter even a squeak as she watched him crossing the space between them. He stopped mere inches away so that she could feel the heat coming off

him, and every frantic breath she took held the scent of
him.

'Or am I getting my signals crossed here? Is it outrage,
Kate, or something else? Wasn't I supposed to take no
for an answer just now? Were you disappointed because
I turned out like all the others? Did you expect me to
follow you in here and take what we both wanted? Is
that it, Kate? No surrender, but to the victor go the
spoils?' Aidan's voice had become low and husky, with
a hint of intimacy that chased shivers along her spine.

She was at once aghast at his misinterpretation and
dismayed at her own inability to move away. Her brain
said move, but her feet seemed rooted. 'I...'

'Yes, Kate? You...what? Want me to kiss you? Is
that it? You want me to storm the citadel and claim it
for my own?'

Dry-mouthed, she took a step away, voice uttering a
husky denial. 'No!'

'I wonder why I don't believe you.' Laughing, he
caught her back with strong hands on her arms. 'I can
feel you trembling, Kate, so I think you're going to have
to prove you mean that.'

Seeing his head lowering, she began to struggle. But
he was too strong and her efforts only half-hearted. A
helpless moan of capitulation broke from her throat.
Then his lips were claiming hers, his arms going about
her to pull her close to the hardness of his body—and
Kate was lost, as she had known she would be. A shudder
of pure pleasure racked her as her breasts came into
contact with the wall of his chest. Her eyes closed and
her head fell back, lips parting to the gliding invasion
of his tongue. Dizzily she met that silken thrust, joining
in an erotic dance that sent spears of flame down through
her to start up a delicious throbbing.

With a sigh, her arms reached up around his neck,
one hand combing into the thick dark hair, fingers tight-

ening convulsively as the kiss went deeper and deeper. The glide of his hands along her spine brought a shiver of delight, and mindlessly she pressed closer still to his blatantly aroused body.

It was Aidan who broke away first, chest heaving as he dragged in air. Bereft, she moaned, and opened her eyes to look up into his face, uncaring that she was revealing all her pent-up longing.

Smouldering eyes locked with hers. 'Where are your claws now, little cat?' he murmured with a husky laugh, and took her parted lips once more.

It wasn't the kiss that triggered off the violent trembling of her body, but the name he called her. Without warning she was catapulted back into that long dark tunnel, nauseated by an overwhelming feeling of disgust and loathing. She was trapped. Oppressed. A force uncaring of her pain, blind to her fear and dread was killing her—killing the woman in her.

She wanted to fight, but she was shaking so badly there was little she could do. With a despairing sob, she kicked out, and the next instant she was falling, finding herself pinned beneath a stifling weight. Her mind went into shock, long shudders of revulsion shaking her slender frame. Turning her head, she stared blindly at the wall, hating the knowledge that she was helpless.

Above her, Aidan went quite still. His body, still pressed so close to hers where they had landed on the bed, couldn't fail to register the tremors that shook her. Shifting on to his elbows, he stared down at her averted face, his own white with shock.

'Kate?' He used a hand to turn her to him. 'What the hell?' His shock was evident as he saw the blank eyes in her pale face. 'My God! Kate! *Kate!*'

From far away she heard her name and she looked up into a face very nearly as white as her own. A serious, concerned face in which a scar stood out sharply. With a choking gasp, time and place returned. This was Aidan, and they were in the hotel. What had she done? But she already knew. It had happened again, just like that day in her office, only much, much worse. Dear God, was she going crazy?

'Let me up!' The frantic command had none of her usual control, and she thought for a panicky moment it was going to be ignored. But then Aidan rolled away to the side and she was free. Without looking at him, she scrambled to her feet with scant dignity. Trembling hands smoothed her dress down, then lifted to check her hair. It hung raggedly about her face, loosened by the struggle, and her nerves jolted.

Biting down hard on her lip, with jerky movements she tried to pin it back, but the pins had vanished and suddenly it was all too much. Tears stung her eyes as she searched the floor. 'Where are the damn pins?' Her voice was a thread away from hysteria and that terrified her into gulping it back.

The bed creaked as Aidan stood up, then he was before her, hand holding out the lost pins. 'Don't panic, they're here.'

'I'm not panicking!' Her eyes shot to his, saw the concern there, and darted away again. 'Thanks.' She took the pins from him, trying to avoid contact.

Unseen by her, Aidan frowned. His hand went to stop her turning away. 'Kate, what——?'

'Don't touch me!' She stepped backwards hastily, terrified that if he did, it would all happen again. Then, realising that she was only making a bad situation worse, she forced herself to be calm. 'Please, don't touch me. I—I couldn't bear it right now.' Going to the nearest mirror, she swiftly put her hair to rights, trying to ignore the other figure reflected behind her that didn't take his eyes off her.

'Kate, we have to talk about this. It's pretty clear something frightened you, but I wasn't about to rape you, whatever you thought. I think I have the right to know what's going on.'

'Rights!' Kate spun round. 'You have no rights over me! No man does! If it comes to rights, then I have the right not to be pawed by you...!' She faltered to a halt. She was over-reacting, his frowning expression told her so. 'Excuse me.' Abruptly she moved across to the bathroom, locking herself in.

Resting her hands on the sink, she took several deep breaths, shudders racking her as, very slowly, she forced herself to calm down. What was happening to her? First the nightmares, and now this. What did it all mean? She covered her face with her hands. They had to be connected, but how? Dear heaven, it was frightening to have this going on inside her and not know what it was all about!

And there was Aidan, demanding explanations. Which she couldn't give because she didn't know herself! How could she explain the inexplicable? She'd have to brazen it out somehow, find a lie he would accept. But what? She bit her lip. If only Rae were here, they could talk it through. Rae cared. Aidan didn't. She couldn't have just anyone poking and prying into her private agonies! She'd just have to survive on her own. But she didn't mind admitting she was scared—scared of what she might uncover.

For now, though, she had to shake it off. There was Aidan to face and the evening to get through. With that in mind she made minor repairs to her make-up, took a steadying breath, and let herself back into the bedroom. A quick glance showed her Aidan was by the window. She had to take control of the situation, bring normality back.

'You'll have to hurry, or we'll be late. I'll be in the other room,' she said calmly.

'Don't for a minute think I've given up, Kate,' he told her as he turned, letting the curtain drop. 'I mean to know.'

Kate paused, summoning up a cool smile. 'Know? I'm sorry, I have no idea what you mean,' she murmured, crossing to the door into the sitting-room.

'I see. Nothing happened. I imagined it all? We weren't making love and you didn't freak out?'

Summoning up her reserves, she faced him fully. 'I didn't "freak out", as you so quaintly put it. I merely put an end to something I found distasteful.' She managed to instil ice into her voice, and was quite pleased with the result. Until Aidan countered after a short silence.

'How distasteful?'

Damn him, why couldn't he just accept it? Now what did she say? 'Frankly, I couldn't stand you touching me,' she invented desperately.

His brows rose and he crossed his arms. 'Is that so?' he asked, silky-smooth.

Alarm shot through her. 'Would I lie to you?' she countered.

He rubbed his chin thoughtfully. 'Now that's an interesting question, isn't it? I'm something of a mean poker player myself. Should I call the bluff? I'll have to think about that one. While I do, you think on this. I can keep running as long as you can. Whatever scared the life out of you isn't going away, and neither am I.' That last statement was punctuated by the bathroom door closing after him, followed by the gush of water.

Kate went into the other room and sank into an armchair, knowing that, far from being over, the real battle was only just starting. He wasn't kidding, and he already knew far too much. Far from being daunted, he had retrieved her mythical gauntlet and taken up the challenge. Now she was locked in a war she had to win and it made her more than ever determined that his curiosity—and that was all it surely could be—wouldn't be satisfied. She was no mean fighter herself, as he was about to find out.

When Aidan walked quietly into the room half an hour later, he found her sitting composedly on the couch flicking through a magazine. Though he hadn't made a noise, Kate's inner radar was ultra-sensitive to his presence, and the nerves in her stomach flip-flopped crazily as she looked up. Their eyes locked in silent battle.

'Ready for the fray?' His tone was cool. Only his eyes gave away the fact that he didn't mean their dinner engagement.

'I just have to collect my coat and bag,' Kate supplied equally coolly, rising gracefully. In the bedroom she quickly glanced in the mirror. Thank God she didn't look as tense as she felt. Gathering up her things, she went to join him.

Mitch and Sarah Norman, a friendly couple in their fifties, were waiting for them in the hotel lounge. Their congratulations were as warm and genuine as they were themselves, and Kate felt a twinge of guilt at deceiving them. A feeling that grew when Sarah handed her a gift-wrapped package as they sat over drinks.

'It's not much,' she excused, 'but when Mitch told me Aidan had just got married, I had to get you something.'

The something turned out to be a crystal goblet, beautifully engraved with their names. Kate felt a lump of emotion grow in her chest. It reminded her of just what a sham this marriage was.

'Come back, Kate,' Aidan's humorous prompt brought her back to the present.

Blinking, she realised they were waiting for her to say something. She produced a smile. 'You really shouldn't have, but thank you. It's quite beautiful. Oh...!' The soft exclamation left her lips as she studied the engraving. 'They've put Katrine.'

'Oh, dear, don't tell me that's wrong! I was sure it was what Aidan told me,' Sarah looked positively crestfallen, and Kate hastened to reassure her.

'It is. It's just that hardly anybody calls me that. I'm just plain old Kate,' she laughed self-consciously.

'But it's such a lovely name!' Sarah exclaimed. 'So feminine. It suits you. Don't you agree, Aidan?' she appealed to the younger man.

Kate just had to look at him, one eyebrow raised tauntingly. He met the challenge by sliding his arm round her waist and bringing a riot of colour to her cheeks in the process. She went rigid, muscles tensing to pull away, when the bite of his fingers on her waist warned her to sit still.

His lips brushed her cheek. 'Act One, Scene One, remember!' he warned her in a sibilant whisper.

She subsided at once, excruciatingly aware of his hand resting so possessively on the curve of her hip. A prickly heat broke out all over her. For all the good it did, the material of her dress might not have been there.

Sensing her acquiescence, Aidan raised his voice. 'I do, as a matter of fact,' he said, eyes locking on the frantic pulse that beat in her neck. 'A graceful name for a graceful lady.'

He sounded so sincere, so convincing, that Kate was startled. Smiling, his eyes held hers. The message was clear and it irritated her. She had to play up, it was all an act. She swayed towards him, smile as warm as a snake. 'Is this good enough for you, darling?' she whispered acidly.

His eyes glittered, and with barely a pause he closed the gap and took a kiss that stole her breath away.

'However,' he went on smoothly as he eased reluctantly away and surveyed the flush on her cheeks with approval, 'There are times when she's most definitely a Kate. I had the devil's own job persuading her to marry me. Didn't I?'

Angry at the triumph she saw in his eyes, she rose swiftly to the bait. 'Are you implying I'm a shrew?' she demanded dulcetly, only her eyes flashing daggers. He responded with a grin.

'I'd be careful how I answered that, Aidan,' Mitch advised with a chuckle. 'People have been known to head for Reno on less provocation.'

'I'm not afraid of Kate,' Aidan replied, returning her stare for stare, and there was something in his tone which said, But I'd love to know what she's afraid of, that put her on her mettle.

'No,' Sarah interjected teasingly. 'We know what you're afraid of, don't we, big baby?'

'Sarah, I swear, if you utter one word, your days are numbered,' Aidan threatened, but the older woman didn't turn a hair.

'Phooey! You're all talk, you men. If I feel like telling Kate, I will. A woman needs all the edge she can get.' She gave Kate a broad wink and turned to her husband. 'When are we going to eat? I'm starving.'

They made a move then. While Mitch paid the bill, Aidan took the goblet to be locked in the safe overnight. That left the two women together. Sarah took Kate's arm as they wandered into the lobby.

'Spiders,' Sarah revealed confidentially. 'Aidan can't stand them. If you don't believe me, just wait until he finds one in the bath! Oh-oh, here they come! Now, remember, don't say a word. Just keep it in mind. You'll know when to use it.'

Kate smiled and forbore to tell her there wouldn't be time because the marriage was only temporary. All the same, it was nice to know he had a weakness.

Dinner, considering the company, should have been a sparkling affair, but Kate found it difficult to relax. It had been an exhausting day, one way or another, and it was draining to have to watch her behaviour. It took all her skill to keep her answers cheerful and her smile in place. It was left up to Aidan to keep the conversational ball rolling, which he did with considerable panache. He revealed an unexpected sense of humour, not unlike her own, and was at times so downright wicked that she had to laugh. But her appetite was small, and she only picked at the meal.

By the time they went on to the nightclub, Kate was definitely feeling the strain, but the other couple had gone to such trouble to give them a good time that she didn't have the heart to say she'd had enough. They drank a champagne toast while the cabaret was on, and then the band struck up and couples took to the floor.

'Kate?' Aidan's hand came to rest on her shoulder. 'Shall we?'

There was no good reason for refusing to dance, and, giving him her hand, she allowed him to help her to her feet and lead her out among the dancing couples.

On the dance-floor, Aidan turned her into his arms. She tried to keep her distance but somehow it just wasn't possible. Nothing seemed important when she was this close to him. Bowing to the inevitable, she closed her eyes, forgetting everything but the pleasure of having his arms close around her. They fitted together perfectly, as if they were made for each other. Within seconds, her body had relaxed, moulding itself to his, feeling every movement as he steered them around the floor, one muscular thigh brushing tantalisingly between hers with every step. The crowd faded away. There were just the two of them.

'Enjoying yourself?' Aidan asked, voice husky, his breath warm on her cheek.

Kate looked up, eyes dreamy, and beyond his head she could see the sky. Blinking, she realised he had steered her out on to the balcony. They were quite alone in the darkness. She didn't answer his question. She couldn't.

A snowflake came to rest on her cheek and melted. He reached up to brush the moisture away gently. 'Oh-oh, Kate, I think the Ice Queen is melting.'

Before she could reply, his mouth brushed hers, and she forgot all she might have said. All she could do was respond mindlessly as he wrought havoc of the most delicious kind with lips and tongue; stroking the sensitive inner skin, teeth nipping at pulsing lips until she moaned and he deepened the kiss, arms drawing her close into the prison of his arms.

When he let her go, she was dazed, and could only stare up at him, seeing the stars glittering in his eyes.

'So,' he murmured huskily, 'you can't bear to have me touch you, eh, Kate?'

Blue eyes rounded as shock tore through her. She tried to break free, but he wouldn't let her. She was obliged to stay where she was, but she refused to look at him as pleasure died inside her.

'Very clever!' she declared huskily.

'I thought so. Hell, Kate, don't be bitter because I called your bluff,' he chided gently.

'Whatever you're trying to do, it won't work,' she shot back, near to tears.

He gave her a small shake. 'Little fool, can't you see I'm only trying to help?'

Stormy-eyed, she stared up at him. 'All I see is curiosity, and I won't pander to that.'

He swore viciously under his breath. 'Why can't I be genuine in my willingness to help?' he demanded.

'Because there's no reason why you should!' she retorted fiercely. 'I'm nothing to you but a convenience. I'm useful and you want me. That's all.'

Anger got the better of him. 'And you want me, don't forget. I could take you to bed and make you tell me,' he threatened in frustration.

She gasped. 'Try it and I'll tell you just one thing. Go to hell!'

'And join you? I don't think I'd like it there!' Aidan said succinctly, and Kate winced at the accuracy of his thrust. 'Kate, you can trust me.'

She shuddered, crazily aware that she wanted to and knowing she couldn't risk it. It added an edge to her voice. 'Trust a Crawford? That'll be the day!'

'You will in the end,' he promised.

She shook him off—or tried to. 'I don't need help, from you or anyone—but especially from you!'

His face tightened with anger. 'OK, if that's the way you want to play it. Remember this, though, there are no rules. The gloves are off. If it gets rough, you've only yourself to blame. Now smile, darling, we're being watched. You love me, remember.'

God, he was hateful! Angrily she plastered a smile on her face as they went inside, and, though it felt stiff and unnatural to her, the Normans didn't see anything wrong. A short time later the party broke up.

Silence reigned in the cab that bore them back to their hotel for their first night together. Turning her head slightly, Kate found she could study his profile. Occasionally his scar caught the light, but funnily enough she generally barely noticed it. There was a strength in his face, and a gentle humour too. He could be angry and mocking, but she had never seen his grey eyes glitter with malice as his brother's did.

Everything pointed to his being a strong man, one you could trust. Had she been wrong to throw that offer back in his face? But she had become used to relying only on herself, of hiding the terrors that stalked her. And she was afraid of pity. She couldn't bear that. So she had to have done the right thing, hadn't she?

A sudden intrusion of light glittered off his eyes, and she realised he was watching her. How long for, and what was he thinking?

'Change your mind, Kate,' he urged softly.

She looked away and hurried into speech. 'I liked Sarah and Mitch.'

He sighed. 'They're nice people.' His voice was pitched low and slightly husky. 'They liked you too, Katrine. Katrine,' he repeated, the word rolling about his tongue. 'Do you know what your name sounds like? The brush of silk on soft scented skin. Katrine.'

Kate smothered a gasp. She had never thought that the mere saying of her name could have so many nuances, and all of them raising the fine hairs on her skin. To combat a sudden breathlessness, she declared, 'I prefer Kate.'

Aidan's bark of laughter was oddly harsh. 'Of course you do.'

'Don't try to seduce me, Aidan,' she warned tautly.

'Could I?' His voice mocked her, and she gritted her teeth.

'I won't fall for that line a second time!'

'Won't you?'

She gasped. 'I hate you!'

'Really? But then, you hate all men, don't you, my little Ice Queen?'

It was a statement, not a question, and one she was grateful not to be obliged to answer, for they drew up outside their hotel. But she was aware of a sharp thrust of pain at his scorn. Because it wasn't true. She didn't

hate him—not all the time. There was just no percentage
in liking him, and falling in love was out of the question.
Not that she was likely to fall in love with him. She wasn't
that stupid!

CHAPTER SEVEN

AS SHE had feared, the nightmare came. It crept into her sleep in the darkest, loneliest hours of the night, when her defences were at their lowest ebb. Now the shadows were gaining substance, and the terror intensified. She was in a room, a strange room dominated by a bed. A room so large she couldn't see the corners, but she knew that something evil lurked in the darkness beyond her vision. And though she knew, she couldn't move to run or fight it off as it came inexorably closer.

Beneath the sheets of the hotel bed, Kate's moans grew increasingly louder, her head thrashing from side to side as she witnessed her dream-self remain still, even though she willed it to move, to run. But there was no escape, and she wept and cried out—a sound to chill the heart. Then, as the oppressive darkness crowded in, she heard her name, faint and far off, but getting stronger, nearer.

'Kate!'

The voice was sharp, the hand on her shoulder imperative. With a gasp she obeyed, opening eyes still dark and haunted by terror. The transition to waking was instant, but the fear remained with her. She saw Aidan sitting on her bed in the low glow of a lamp, his hand still on her shoulder, and her heart jerked.

'What?' The sound was thready and fearful.

Aidan frowned, grey eyes reflecting concern. 'You called out in your sleep. You were crying.'

Her hand went to her cheek, feeling the moisture there. 'Oh, God!' The thing she had feared most had happened. She drew in a shaky breath. 'I'm sorry I woke you.'

He let that pass, eyes watchful. 'That was some nightmare you were having. I take it you've had it before?'

'Yes.' She ran a hand through her hair. It was damp with sweat, and the silk pyjamas she had put on earlier were clinging uncomfortably to her skin. It had been a bad one tonight, and the awful thing was that it was becoming clearer. Each night there was more revealed, and the fear grew apace with it. Shivering in reaction, Kate sat up against the pillows and closed her eyes. How much more could she take? These dreams were heading her somewhere, and she was scared, really scared of what she might discover.

She flicked a glance at Aidan, caught the glow of the lamp on his naked chest and hastily looked away. Tonight they had shared a room, and she had seen so much more in her dreams. Could there be a connection? Those other incidents—once he had touched her, the other he had used that name. Perhaps it was only coincidence, but something was happening. Yet, undeniably, twice he had called her back from the edge of something too terrible. Lord, how she wished she understood!

Licking her lips, she looked at him once more. 'I'll be all right now,' she lied, knowing it was doubtful if she'd sleep again tonight.

'Sure you will,' he agreed sceptically. 'I'll get you some water.' He disappeared into the bathroom and was back again in seconds with a tumbler. Handing it to her, he resumed his seat, watching as she drained it. 'Feeling better?' He relieved her of the glass and set it aside. 'Care to talk about it? Something must have triggered it off.'

Still strung out, she very nearly laughed. Her husband was the last person with whom she could ever discuss her bad dreams. How could she say, 'I think it's you,' when she still couldn't explain it herself? So instead she lied. 'There wouldn't be much point. Once I wake up, it's gone.'

'You were struggling as if your life depended on it when I tried to wake you. What were you protecting so fiercely?'

Drawing up her knees, she propped her head on them. 'I told you, I don't remember,' she gritted through her teeth. A sudden welling of hot tears stung the back of her eyes. 'I don't remember,' she added despairingly.

Watching her downbent head, Aidan chose his next words carefully. 'Do you want to?' he asked gently.

She looked up, eyes wild. 'Have you been sent to torment me?'

His eyes narrowed. 'Is that what you think?'

'I don't know! I don't know anything any more. I don't...' she dropped her head '...think you'd better take any notice of me. I'm so tired. So very, very tired. This isn't me talking. You know it isn't.' Her voice fell to a whisper he had to strain to hear. 'Don't nightmares ever end?'

'The night-time ones, almost always.'

'But they don't. They don't,' she contradicted brokenly.

Sighing, he brushed the hair from where it clung to her cheek. 'This one has, for now. Go to sleep, Kate, you're burned out. There's nothing to fear. I'm here. You're not alone now.'

Not alone. It sounded so good. She'd been alone for such a long time now. Her eyes probed his for long seconds before finally she lay down again, hugging the covers to her chin. She looked at him in confusion. 'Why are you being kind to me?'

Standing up, he switched off the light. 'Everyone deserves a little kindness sometimes, Kate.' His voice reached her through the darkness. 'Go to sleep.'

Kate closed her eyes, not expecting to sleep, but it rolled over her in waves, and this time there were no dreams to disturb her. It was Aidan who lay awake in the darkness thinking.

The next time Kate stirred, pale winter sunlight was filtering through a crack in the heavy curtains. Brushing the hair from her eyes, she focused on the clock. It showed a little after nine. Her first thought was that she was late for work, then memory returned, and she quickly glanced over her shoulder at the other bed. It was empty, and she subsided with a sigh of relief.

She was glad of these moments alone to get her thoughts together. The nightmare was as vivid as always, but so were other, more disturbing things. She remembered Aidan and his unexpected kindness—and, more uncomfortably, she recalled the things she had said. How could she have been so stupid? Now he was no longer guessing, he knew something was wrong. What sort of feeble idiot did he think she was now, unable to cope with a bad dream?

It was with a crawling sense of embarrassment that Kate showered and dressed in tailored black trousers and a burgundy sweater. Every time she thought of what had passed, she cringed, and that made her furious with herself. She was just zipping on a pair of high-heeled ankle-boots when Aidan appeared in the doorway. She glanced up and in silence they stared at each other while the heat rose in her cheeks.

'Good morning,' he greeted gently.

In her sensitive state, she fancied she saw pity in his eyes, and, immediately defensive, she snapped back, 'Is it?' and glanced away.

Unseen, his brows rose. 'I've seen worse for the time of year.'

She refused to look at him. 'Really?'

Now his lips did curve. 'What's the matter, Kate?' That question, too, was gentle.

A lump rose in her throat. 'Nothing. I overslept, and I don't like it. You should have woken me.' With nowhere else to go, her anger was channelled towards him.

Aidan merely shrugged. 'There's no rush. The snow stopped during the night, so, providing we don't leave it too late, we should make Washington without any trouble. I ordered breakfast. Ten minutes, OK?'

'Fine,' she said shortly. Did he have to be so cheerful? Why couldn't he be distant or angry? Angry was much better. 'I'll be there. I've almost finished, but I'll get on faster with you out of the way!'

Unperturbed, he laughed. 'That sounds like my marching orders. Oh, and by the way, I like your hair like that. It's softer. It suits you.' With another brief smile he disappeared again.

Bemused, she stared after him, then, irritated out of all proportion by her reaction, she tugged at the zipper, caught her finger in the teeth, and swore, pungently. Stomping over to the mirror, she glared at her reflection. Her hair hung about her face in a silver cloud. She had brushed it till it shone, but hadn't pinned it up. Yes, it looked softer, but it made her face look vulnerable. So he liked it, did he? Why? Because he thought she was a soft touch after last night? Ready to reveal everything? Well, he was damn well wrong! With angry movements she pinned every last wisp of it back into its pleat.

Keeping her make-up to a minimum, Kate walked into the sitting-room just as the breakfast trolley was being wheeled in. As she seated herself at the table by the window, she was aware of Aidan's quizzical glance at her hair, but he said nothing until they were alone.

'I suppose if I'd said I liked it pinned up, you'd have let your hair hang free, you perverse little madam!' he mocked derisively.

Because it was all too true, her reply was short and snappy. 'Not at all. Nothing you said would influence me one way or another. I happen to like my hair up. It keeps it out of the way while I'm working.'

'Ah, I see,' Aidan murmured as he poured coffee for them both. 'But you're not working now,' he pointed out reasonably. 'So why don't you let it down?'

'Because...' she began, only to falter at the challenging look in his eye. For no accountable reason, her heart kicked.

A slow smile curved his lips. 'Because then you wouldn't look like the woman you want me to believe you are?' he supplied for her.

Now she knew she was right to be worried. How he had arrived at that deduction, she had no idea, but that he had was alarming enough. This had to stop now. She forced a laugh from her tight throat. 'You're being ridiculous,' she informed him, reaching for her coffee. 'A hairstyle is a hairstyle.'

'And a fraud is a fraud.'

The cup she had been raising to her lips almost fell from her nerveless fingers, and she set it down hastily. 'Fraud?' She strove to be casual, but somehow it came out on a quaver. She would have got up and walked out if there had been any strength in her legs, but as it was she had to remain and face this startling turn of events.

Aidan helped himself to ham and eggs before carrying on. 'I did some serious thinking last night, after your nightmare,' he revealed, bringing colour to her pale cheeks.

Kate saw a means of diverting him and jumped at it. 'Actually, I was meaning to talk to you about that,' she interrupted swiftly.

He looked up. 'Really? You're not eating. Aren't you hungry?'

She automatically reached for a slice of toast, feeling she was being reeled in by an expert. Abandoning the food to her plate, she took a deep breath and tried again. 'I wanted to apologise for disturbing you. I think I made rather a fool of myself.'

'Do you?'

It wasn't a statement she'd expected to be questioned, even as mildly as he did, and it put her right off balance. 'Don't you?' she snapped.

Aidan shook his head. 'No.'

Feeling hounded, Kate threw up her hands. 'I don't understand you!' she cried.

If it was possible for a broad smile to broaden, his did then. 'That's a pity, because I think I'm beginning to understand you.'

Icy fingers of warning chased their way along her spine. 'I don't want you to understand me,' she declared through her teeth, and then could have bitten her tongue out at the impulsively revealing words.

'I know you don't, but I told you yesterday you couldn't stop me,' he told her while munching on some toast. Kate, appetite vanishing, watched him, feeling vaguely nauseous. 'Want to know what I came up with?'

'No,' she rejoined pointedly, hands clenching into fists. 'But somehow I don't think that's going to stop you telling me.'

His laugh was appreciative. 'You see, you do understand me after all. But we were talking about you, Kate. Not only are you a fraud, but you're an illusionist too. The swiftness of the tongue deceives the eye.'

Expecting more along lines that already set her nerves jangling, Kate was surprised when he stopped. 'Is that it?' she demanded in disbelief.

'There is one other thing,' he informed her ominously.

'And that is?'

'I think you ought to know that I don't believe the Ice Queen exists.'

Shocked, her mouth went dry. 'You know she does. You've seen her yourself,' she insisted, fighting a desperate rearguard battle for her defences—her only defences.

Aidan shook his head. 'Perhaps she did, but not any more. Oh, she tries to. Every now and again when you're under threat, there she is, but you can't maintain it. So why don't you let her go, Kate? You don't need her any more,' he urged gently.

'I do——'

'No you don't,' he interrupted. 'She's lost her street credibility, at least with me. You may have needed her once. I don't believe you need her now, unless you think I'm a real threat, and I'm not, Kate. Hopefully, you'll soon come to believe me.'

'And then what?' she croaked, helplessly.

'Then, my dear Kate, we can begin to help you.'

Her hands balled into fists. 'I've told you——'

'And I've heard you. Think about it. Don't make any quick decisions. Forget the past. Start here and now.'

Kate stared at him, unsure just what was going on behind that charming face. Overnight he had changed tack, leaving her floundering helplessly in his wake. She was a good swimmer, but suddenly she seriously doubted that that would be enough. Yet she had to try, for pride, if nothing else. How bitterly she regretted that lapse last night, for she was paying for it now.

'I don't understand why you're doing this,' she observed shakily, striving for normality by sipping at her coffee and grimacing at its cold bitterness.

Obligingly, Aidan poured her a fresh cup. 'I know, but you will in time.'

Hot coffee went a long way to restoring her equilibrium. 'On the whole, I think I prefer you ranting and raving at me.'

'Of course you do,' he agreed easily, 'but that's because people in a temper very rarely see further than the end of their own anger.'

'I think you're a very devious, dangerous man,' Kate declared with a sense of being caught tighter and tighter in a trap.

Aidan merely smiled that enigmatic smile that was beginning to grate on her nerves. 'Remind me to tell you about Abraham Lincoln some time.' Draining the dregs from a second cup of coffee, he pushed himself to his feet. 'I'm going to pack while you finish your breakfast. I've ordered a hire car for ten-thirty.' He stopped behind her as he passed. 'On second thoughts, keep your hair up, Kate. I've just discovered you've got a deliciously inviting nape.'

Before she had any idea of what he intended to do, he had done it. Warm lips brushed the tender cord. Kate gasped as tiny electric shocks tingled down her spine, creating havoc with her breathing. She jerked away, and Aidan uttered a husky laugh.

'Just checking,' he excused himself, and went on his way.

At the table, Kate sagged in her seat, feeling drained. She couldn't believe what she had just been through. She had a panicky sense of having walked into the wrong play, where, though everything looked familiar, she had no idea what was going on. Which wasn't strictly true. She had created a mystery and he wanted to solve it. This was just another try from a different angle. Like his seduction number last night. Well, she was forewarned now, and wasn't about to fall for it. She wasn't a source of free entertainment!

And yet... He had sounded so sincere. She groaned aloud. What on earth was she going to do?

It had snowed quite heavily overnight, but the snow-ploughs had been out on the highways and they had no trouble leaving the city and heading for the capital. The car was a Mercedes and very luxurious, and Kate was content to simply sit back in comfort and watch the world go by. Aidan was a good driver, taking account of the conditions, and she felt perfectly safe with him.

It was a novel sensation, and her mind dwelt on it as she looked out at the snowy landscape. It gave her other things to consider. If she felt safe with him, could she also trust him? More importantly perhaps, would she respond as she did to someone who was basically untrustworthy? She didn't think so. But emotions were fickle; they didn't need only good ground in which to grow. So how on earth was she to decide who to trust— and did she really want to? If only she knew why he was really doing this. What did he want of her? What did *she* want of him? Why were there only questions and no answers?

She tried to think of something else, but that merely replaced one anxiety with another. The meeting with his father and stepmother was not one she was looking forward to. There was just no way she could imagine them welcoming her, knowing who she was and what she had done. All right, she was making amends, but that would hardly endear her to them.

Feeling the tension starting to mount as the miles ticked past, she sought for another diversion, and said the first thing that came into her head. 'You were going to tell me about the President.'

So abruptly did she break the silence that had settled about them that it had Aidan's head snapping round, and very nearly deposited them in the ditch.

Muttering curses under his breath, he straightened the car. 'For God's sake! What were you trying to do? Kill us both?'

Alarm at how close they had come to a real accident made her snappy. 'Perish the thought!'

'Perish is right!' he growled back instantly, then sighed. 'Now what's this about Bush?'

'Not Bush. President Lincoln.'

'Lincoln?' She could see him frown, then the moment light dawned. 'Abraham Lincoln! Ah!' A smile curved his lips. 'Abraham Lincoln, Kate, was a wiry little terrier. He stood so high, but he had a bark like a wolfhound. We got him from the SPCA. He'd been badly mistreated by his owner, but instead of cowering, as you might expect, he'd come out snapping and snarling. You see, he didn't trust anybody, so he attacked everyone. But his eyes... You could see in his eyes that he wanted to be loved. He wanted someone to say, Hey, I don't care how much you bite, I'm going to love you anyway. That's why I took him home. We had some royal battles, but in the end he accepted me and trusted me.'

Kate listened in stricken silence, a huge lump of emotion filling her chest. There was a warmth in his voice that curled fingers about her heart—choking her so that she couldn't breathe.

'Stop the car!' she ordered hoarsely.

Aidan shot her an alarmed glance. 'What's wrong?'

Wrong? 'Just stop the damn car!' she ordered again, and when he pulled over to the side of the road her fumbling fingers found the catch, and she stumbled out into the cold, biting air. Huddling her coat about her, she took a couple of slithery steps away from the car and drew in air in a gulp.

Snow crunched underfoot, but she didn't need that to tell her Aidan had joined her. The hairs on her neck were already at attention. 'What are you trying to do to me?' The words were broken, painful.

Hands stuffed into the pockets of his fleecy-lined denim jacket, Aidan eyed her back watchfully. His breath froze in the air as he said slowly, 'I'm trying to get you to trust me, so that I can help you. I told you about Abe because you're so like him. You strike out, snapping and snarling, making everyone think you're wild and vicious. When all you're really doing is protecting yourself behind a mask.'

Kate paled. It was as if he could really see inside her, see things that nobody else did. He was stripping her layer by layer, leaving her with the frightening feeling that nothing was safe from him. There was no secret he wouldn't find. No truth he wouldn't unveil.

With a heavy sigh, Aidan reached out his hands and turned her round. His face was pale and full of gentle concern. 'Kate, you've got to trust somebody some time.'

She shrugged him off. 'Why can't you just let me be?'

'Because I've never been the sort to pass by on the other side.'

'Try it once, you could get to like it!' she riposted like a ricochet, knowing she was losing ground to his gentleness.

Aidan half smiled. 'Snap away. I've got thick skin.'

He was telling her!

She looked helplessly up at his grimly determined face. He wasn't going to give up! He'd work on her like that dog until he'd won her over!

Gentle fingers reached up to brush a tendril of hair from her eyes. 'Whatever it is, Kate, you don't have to face it on your own any more.'

Her throat closed over. Oh, God, why had he had to say that? Lord knew she had had enough. It was so tempting to give in to the sound of his voice and the look in his eyes. She was so tired of fighting this fear on her own. Why fight it? Why not, just once, lean on someone who was stronger than her? She dropped her lids over gritty eyes. 'All right,' she said in a small, defeated voice.

For a brief moment Aidan closed his eyes and breathed in deeply. When he looked at her again, his expression was cautious. 'Do you want to sit in the car?'

Kate shook her head, knowing she would have to speak now or she would lose her nerve. 'No.' She turned away, pulling her collar up about her ears. Her eyes travelled over the frozen beauty of the winter landscape. 'There's not much to tell, not really. I have these...nightmares. You know that. At first I couldn't remember what happened in them, I only knew the fear I felt.' She swallowed hard. It was painful to reveal it all. 'They started from nowhere.'

'Not nowhere. Wasn't it when you met me?'

The soft question drew her round, her eyes large in her pale face. 'Yes. How...?'

'I'm not blind, Kate. I've seen the changes this past week,' Aidan supplied. 'But that's not all, is it?'

'No,' she agreed huskily and cleared her throat. 'They've started to become much clearer. Each time there's more.' She shuddered, and at once he closed the distance between them and enclosed her in the strength of his arms.

She didn't even think of fighting him.

'Tell me.'

She closed her eyes, hand clutching the cloth of his jacket. 'I feel fear. I can't see it, but it's there, oppressing me. I want to run, but I can't. I'm trapped in a large room and all I can see is me and a bed. Oh, God! I want to run so badly, but I can't. It's...horrible!' She shuddered violently.

'Ssh.' His hand came up to stroke her hair. 'Poor Kate, no wonder you're scared. You shouldn't have kept this to yourself for so long.'

'I thought it was only the dreams, but... I'm seeing things in the daytime too. Oh, God, Aidan, it frightens me so.' She looked up at him in undisguised anguish. 'Am I going crazy?'

'No!' he denied forcefully. 'Don't ever think that. I'm no psychiatrist, Kate, but it seems to me that the dreams are your subconscious mind's way of revealing something you've blocked out. If I'm right, it must have been something pretty bad for you to blank it out. I know you're frightened, but it's something you're going to have to face in order to heal. I'd like you to see... a friend of mine. You'll like her. I've never known her to be anything but kind and understanding. I think she'll confirm what I've said, but, whatever the outcome, you won't be facing it alone, Kate. I'll be with you every step of the way.'

Her eyes probed his. 'How can you say that when this marriage is only temporary?' The thought brought a dart of pain to the region of her heart.

His arms tightened. 'I have no intention of abandoning you, Kate.'

She looked away, resting her head on his shoulder, enjoying the sheer male smell of him as she breathed in. It felt so right, so good. Yet she feared to trust it. 'I don't know why you're doing this.'

'Does there have to be a motive? Do you always suspect everyone? People do do things purely out of a sincere wish to help.'

'Not in my experience,' she said painfully.

'That was unfortunate.' He sighed. 'This is different.'

'How can I be sure of that?'

'Because your instincts tell you to trust me.'

He was right, they did. Why else did it feel so comfortable and safe in his arms? She couldn't ever remember feeling so protected. After years of fighting in the wilderness, it felt so good to surrender her arms. She had found that magical peace she hadn't even known she was searching for.

'Kate, do you think you were raped?'

The soft question brought her head up, breaking the spell. 'Raped? I...don't know.' Could she have been? But surely if she had, she wouldn't respond to Aidan as she did, would she?

'Never mind, it just seemed to fit what you've told me. Forget it for now. Just remember, you don't have to be afraid alone. I'll help you, Kate. You have my solemn promise.' He smiled down at her.

The warmth she saw made her feel strange inside. Uncertain, and suddenly embarrassed at the way she was still clinging to him, Kate stepped back. 'Don't make promises you can't keep,' she advised stiffly.

He turned her round, the arm he placed about her shoulder pointing her towards the car. 'When you know me better, you'll know I never do,' he said calmly.

Vitally aware of the solid strength of him, Kate chewed her lip. Did she want to know him better? Right this second she didn't feel she knew anything—except that she felt strangely bereft when he removed his arm to allow her to get into the car again.

Seconds later they were on their way again. Kate sat in silence, her mind going over all that had happened. Trust him, he said. There were no strings. Yet there had to be a motive. Nobody made the kind of commitment he just had without reason. Or did they? Were her suspicions a hangover from the old Kate? What did she know of him? Only his anger. Perhaps this wasn't out of character for him. Perhaps she ought to revise her opinion of him. After all, that was based on her own

misconceptions. So wouldn't it be wise to suspend
judgement and wait and see what happened next?

Yes, that was what she would do. Besides, she needed
the breathing-space. So much had happened so quickly
that she sometimes felt in a permanent daze. With any
luck she might also find out what it was about him that
made her react to him the way she did. She needed to
know that, desperately.

They stopped for a late lunch at a restaurant that
seemed straight out of Washington Irving. Kate could
feel the atmosphere in the genuine oak beams and lat-
ticed windows, and for no accountable reason felt all the
tension ease away.

'I thought you'd appreciate it,' Aidan declared,
watching her take it all in.

She smiled back at him. 'Oh, I do. It's lovely. Do you
come here often?'

'I try to when I visit Dad. If you like, I can show you
some of the sights of Washington while we're here.'

'I thought you'd have work to do.' Surprise mingled
with a wave of pleasure.

Aidan shrugged. 'Nothing that can't wait. So, what
do you say?'

'I say yes, thank you. I'd love that,' she responded
without hesitation, but the warmth in his eyes made her
suddenly self-conscious, and she looked down at her
drink, confused by new and conflicting emotions.

The meal was as good as the atmosphere suggested,
and Kate found herself relaxing more and more as she
listened to Aidan talking. Her eyes were drawn to him
constantly, eating up every expression. She found herself
laughing at the tales he told her of holidays in the
Adirondacks, even joining in with one or two stories of
her own. She enjoyed his amusement. Aidan had a deep,
warm laugh that set his eyes alight and took years off

him. Kate was fascinated by the swiftly changing moods that crossed his face as he spoke.

She knew he was talking to put her at her ease, and she was grateful, but as time passed she forgot even that. He was weaving a spell about her that made the cold outside disappear, shrinking the world to the golden circle of light thrown by the lamp above them. She could have stayed there forever, watching his hands as they moved to illustrate his point. The intrusion of the real world, via the latest weather forecast, made her feel she was losing something special.

Sitting in the car on the final leg of the journey, she found her eyes still drawn to him as he concentrated on his driving. A stray lock of hair had fallen over his brow and she automatically reached out and brushed it back. He flicked her a glance then, and smiled, and her heart turned over.

She returned her glance to the world outside, heart beating erratically. Dear heaven, it would be so easy to fall in love with him. It was a statement that set her on a seesaw of emotions. She couldn't have already done so, could she? Was that what all this was about? All the swings of mood, the uncertainty and confusion? She'd never been in love, so she didn't know. Wouldn't it be the height of insanity to love Aidan Crawford?

Her eyes sought their reflection in the glass. Was it already too late?

By mid-afternoon they had reached Washington. His father and stepmother lived in the suburbs, in a large, rambling house set in its own grounds. They must have been listening out for the car, for no sooner had Aidan parked in the driveway than the front door opened and three dogs rushed out, closely followed by two humans.

While Aidan dealt with a more vociferous welcome, it was left up to his father to help Kate from the car. Which he did with a smile in which she could detect no hint of reserve. He was a tall man, like his son. In fact, the likeness was striking. Except that Aidan Crawford Senior's hair was pure white. This, Kate thought, is what Aidan will look like in years to come, and the thought was oddly comforting.

'So, you're Kate,' his father declared with a curious glint in his eye, not unreminiscent of his son. 'You stirred up a fine hornets' nest, young lady.'

Kate flushed to the roots of her hair. 'I know. I'm sorry. I ought to explain——'

'No need,' he cut her off. 'You had your reasons. If Aidan knows and understands, that's good enough for us. Welcome to the family.' He proceeded to kiss her on both cheeks.

'Yes indeed, you're very welcome, Kate,' his wife Netta added, but Kate knew instantly that the woman wasn't as sure as the man that her presence was a good thing. She was reserving judgement. Something Kate could fully understand and accept. Nevertheless, she received a swift hug from the woman who, though neat as a pin and with salt and pepper hair, barely reached Kate's shoulder.

'It's freezing out here,' Netta hurried on, taking Kate's arm. 'I'll take Kate inside and make some tea while you deal with the luggage.' She gave her new daughter-in-law a conspiratorial wink. 'They'll turn up in half an hour or so, knowing them, but I don't propose to freeze to death. We'll leave them to it. Aidan tells me you run your own modelling agency. That must be fascinating.'

Thirty minutes later, when indeed the men did finally come in, Kate and Netta were on their second cup of tea before a blazing fire in the sitting-room. Conversation had been easy, for Netta had the knack of putting people at their ease. However, Kate knew she hadn't imagined that hint of reserve, though she hadn't met it again. She realised that Netta's protective instinct was strong, but, as Aidan had said, she was prepared to give the younger woman the benefit of the doubt.

'Any chance of some of that for us?' Aidan Senior asked as he came to toast his hands over the flames.

Netta stood up. 'I'll make some fresh. What did you do with the dogs?'

'Shut up in the den. Aidan didn't know if Kate liked them,' he called after his wife, then turned to his daughter-in-law. 'How are you with dogs, Kate? I hope to God you're as daft about them as my son is. All three are his.'

Kate moved up as Aidan came to sit beside her on the couch. 'We always had dogs when Philip was alive.'

Aidan Senior nodded. 'Ah, yes, your brother. That was a sorry business, Kate. I liked your father very much. You have my assurance that, had I known, I would most certainly have helped. Cold comfort, I know. I can only apologise for Andrew. I'm afraid there's a devil in him that *I* could never control, and *he* was never willing to try to. His mother and I divorced when the boys were quite young. It seemed the ideal arrangement to take one each. Andrew was her favourite, and that was his undoing. She never could curb his excesses, and now, of course, it's much too late. You could say I got the better bargain. Aidan was easy to raise, never giving me a day's worry more than a growing boy should. But it's the weak who really need our help, not the strong. I'll always wonder if Andrew might have turned out differently if he had come to me.'

'He would only have pretended to change,' his son put in wryly. 'And that would have been worse, Dad. You can't blame yourself for anything. He was just born wild.'

Aidan Senior came and laid a hand on his son's shoulder, squeezing firmly. 'I know, son. We all love him, and make excuses. But one day, mark my words,

he'll go too far, and do something that we can't forgive
him for. I'll tell you now, it's not a day I look forward
to.' He sighed heavily, looked at Kate and smiled. 'But
we were talking about the dogs. You'll like these. All of
them are daft as a brush. Get Aidan to introduce you
to them later, then we'll let them loose.'

Netta returned then, carrying a fresh tray of tea, and
overheard the last part of the conversation. 'The only
thing you need worry about is that they'll lick you to
death!' she declared drily. 'By the way, Aidan, we've put
you in the main guest room. It will be yours and Kate's
room now. We've moved most of your things across,
but we've left you to arrange it how you like.'

Kate felt the tension in Aidan immediately, but when
she glanced at him he was smiling. 'Thanks, Netta. I'll
have that tea first, then we'll go up and unpack.'

A quarter of an hour later, he led the way upstairs,
carrying their cases. Outside one door, he stopped and
set down a case, reaching for the handle. He paused then,
giving her a long sideways look before shrugging mentally and swinging the door open.

'This is our room,' he said in a curiously flat tone,
and stood back to allow her to precede him.

Already tense from picking up the vibrations from
him, Kate stepped inside, and knew immediately why he
had been acting so strangely. It was a beautiful room,
decorated in cheery spring tones, but there was only one
bed.

Behind her, Aidan set the cases down and closed the
door. 'I'm afraid I hadn't given much thought to the
sleeping arrangements once we got here. But I'm sure
you know you have nothing to fear from me. As you
can see, it's a big bed. We won't even have to touch.'

'No, we won't,' she agreed as she crossed to the
window, pretending to take an interest in the snow-
covered grounds. It wasn't fear that dried her mouth at

the thought of sharing the bed with him, but something
that set her heart beating erratically in her chest. In the
glass, she saw Aidan come up behind her. Saw his hands
lift, then hesitate a second before he rested them lightly
on her shoulders. Their warmth seeped into her, relaxing
the tension in her muscles. Their eyes locked in the glass.
He smiled and she gave in to the temptation to lean back
against him. Only his fingers tightened abruptly, halting
the movement before they could touch.

'You know, in days gone by, a knight would lay his
sword down the middle of the bed as his pledge of
honour,' he told her in a low voice.

There was something in his tone that made her stiffen.
'What are you trying to say?'

Aidan released her, hands thrusting into his pockets
as she turned round. 'I guess I'm trying, not very clearly,
to say that you needn't fear I'll try to make love to you.'

A hot tide of embarrassment stained her cheeks. 'Oh,
I see.' Ducking her head, she brushed past him, going
to their cases. What a fool! What an idiot! How obtuse
could she be? He was trying to tell her he wasn't interested. As kindly as he could, considering she had virtually issued a silent invitation. Kindness, she knew now,
was one of his strong points. It wasn't his fault she had
embarrassed herself. Nor could he know how that gentle
rejection hurt.

She rallied quickly, but her laugh had a brittle quality.
'Well, that's a load off my mind. Now I'd better unpack.
I'll do yours for you too, if you like,' she gabbled to
hide the fact that something inside her had suffered a
deep wound.

Behind her, Aidan gave her an odd look as he lifted
his case on to the bed. 'Thanks, I'll take you up on that.
I hate unpacking.' With a smile he left her to it.

Kate slumped down on to the bed as the door closed
behind him. Aidan was treating her like a big brother,

and instead of being relieved she felt cheated. She didn't want a brother, she wanted . . . A moan escaped her. Oh, lord, she *had* fallen in love with him. Friendship wasn't enough—not nearly enough! She wanted everything from him, no half measures. The depth of her feeling was shocking. How had it happened so quickly?

She didn't know, she only knew it was so, and that in the face of his brotherliness it was hopeless. He didn't want her and the wisest thing she could do was follow his lead and salvage a little of her pride. She might have done a foolish thing, but she needn't compound it by letting him know.

They took the dogs for a walk after dinner, and returned to mugs of hot chocolate and marshmallow. It had been an exhausting day, and in no time Kate was almost nodding over her drink. She didn't protest when Aidan drew her to her feet, but wished his parents goodnight and followed him from the room.

In their bedroom, Aidan gathered up his robe. 'You take the bathroom, I'll use the one down the hall.'

Kate watched him go out again with mixed emotions. He was being thoughtful, and she knew she should be grateful, but the fact was she wasn't. It was a hopeless situation. So funny, she'd end up crying in a minute! Biting down hard on her lip, she gathered up her nightdress and headed for the bathroom.

She hoped to have been in bed before Aidan returned, but he was already there when she stepped out of the bathroom. Her stomach clenched on a scalding wave of desire as she saw him relaxed against the pillows, naked to the waist.

She must have paled because Aidan's tone was sharp as he said her name. She stared into her husband's concerned grey eyes.

'Are you OK?' he asked, making to get out of the bed.

'Of course,' she said swiftly, stalling the movement.

'I thought you'd had one of those flashes,' he went on.

Flustered, she made a business of hanging up her clothes. 'No. My head thumped, that was all. It's probably just a headache,' she lied.

It took all of her nerve to cross to the bed and climb beneath the covers as if she hadn't a care in the world. Stiff with tension, she lay as far away from him as she could, lest she betrayed herself by touching him as she longed to do. She held her breath when the bed rocked as Aidan turned the light out. Ears straining in the darkness, she waited for the change in his breathing as he fell asleep. Only then did she begin to relax, despairing that she would ever be able to sleep herself. But her exhausted body took charge at last, drawing her over the edge into an uneasy sleep.

Her own scream woke her hours later, and she found herself sitting up in the darkness, shaking as with an ague, tears streaming down her face.

Everything seemed to happen at once. Beside her, Aidan was shaken into immediate wakefulness, hand shooting out to switch on the light as he too sat up. As he did so, the door burst open, showing his father and Netta framed in the doorway, their faces wearing identical expressions of shock and alarm.

Still shaking, Kate dropped her head in her hands and turned to him. Aidan's arms enclosed her at once. Over her shoulder he glanced at his father and stepmother.

'Good lord, Aidan, what happened? Is Kate all right?' Netta's voice was shaken.

'It's a nightmare. She's had them before,' Aidan explained shortly.

'Is there anything we can do, son?' his father asked, frowning in concern.

'Thanks, Dad, but I don't think so. We can cope. You go back to bed.'

'Well, all right, but you know where I am if you need me,' Netta offered.

They left reluctantly, leaving the couple on the bed alone.

At once Kate groaned. 'Oh, God!' she choked out huskily.

'You screamed. Can you remember why?'

She shuddered. 'He was laughing,' she admitted sickly, recalling it all.

'He?' Aidan prompted. 'Kate, you've got to tell me who,' he urged.

'I don't know who... I couldn't see. It's all... bits. I remember stairs...and laughter. Gloating, horrible...a man's laugh. Oh, God!' she sobbed into his shoulder.

'It's OK. It's OK. It's over now,' he soothed her like a child.

Swallowing hard, she found some control. 'I'm scared. What does it mean?'

'I don't know, Kate. I only wish I did, so I could spare you this.' His voice was a groan muffled by her hair.

Kate slipped her arms around his waist. 'Hold me. Don't let me go,' she pleaded raggedly.

'I won't, sweetheart. Hush now, don't cry any more.' He lay down with her in his arms, pulling the covers up over them, then finally switching off the light.

For Kate the minutes seemed to go by like hours, but slowly the tremors began to die away, until finally they stopped altogether. She was aware of the warmth that came from him seeping into her rigid muscles, easing their awful tension. Occasionally a shudder would rack her, but they, too, became less frequent. She became aware of his heart beating solidly under her ear, a steady, comforting sound. She wanted it never to end. She wanted to stay in his arms forever. If only he could love her as she loved him. If only... A tiny sighing breath escaped her lips, and her fingers slowly uncurled. Her eyelids dropped.

She slipped into sleep with a soft whimper that reminded the man who held her of a lost child. Heaving a deep sigh, he closed his own eyes at last.

CHAPTER EIGHT

KATE stirred with a wonderful feeling of warmth and security. The reason for it eluded her until she sighed and stretched, and became aware of the warm body pressed close to hers. She remembered then the nightmare, and how Aidan had comforted her until she had fallen asleep in his arms.

A slow smile spread across her lips, she felt comfortable, protected—safe in a way she had never experienced before. Some time during the night they had moved, and now they lay spoon-fashion, his arm a pleasurable weight about her waist. She knew she ought to move, but she wanted to savour this moment for as long as possible. Fantasise a little that he held her like this because he loved her. She felt ready to purr, and like a cat, had an instinctive desire to curl up and go to sleep again.

Only it wasn't to be. Behind her Aidan stirred. His arm tightened fractionally about her and her heart skipped a beat as she heard him give a satisfied sigh.

'Mmm, this is nice,' he murmured, voice still husky from sleep.

It brought goose-pimples out on her flesh, and a resurgence of that flash-flood wave of desire. It also brought a swift dart of pain, because clearly he didn't recall who he was holding so tightly. The danger was that she wanted to stay there, pretend he did know. But it was a destructive temptation that could only embarrass them both. So she swallowed hard and did the only thing she could.

'I think I'd better get up,' she suggested, sounding just as husky as he did.

Expecting him to let her go immediately, having recognised her voice, it was a shock when he merely groaned, moving closer. 'Do you want to? Myself, I could stay like this for ever.'

Her eyes rounded like saucers. It wasn't fair that he should tempt her so. Gritting her teeth, she made herself go rigid. 'Aidan! This is me, Kate, remember!' she pointed out tautly.

Sighing, he came up on one elbow to look down at her. 'I remember,' he murmured, sleepy eyes roving warmly over her, starting up flash-fires that pinkened her cheeks. 'Good morning.'

Oh, lord, why did he have to have eyes you could drown in? She couldn't think of one sensible thing to say.

'Lost your tongue?' he teased, smiling easily.

Bewildered, she lay transfixed, quite forgetting all the reasons why she should move. 'This is silly.'

His eyes grew warmer. 'That's not the adjective I'd use. Do you know, you're a very cosy armful, Kate Crawford?'

Her heart started a reckless beat. 'No, but you hum it and I'll join in,' she quipped breathlessly.

He laughed, a sound that warmed her to the core. 'Ah, Kate, you're a woman after my own heart. I knew I couldn't be wrong. Where have you been all my life?'

Perhaps it was reckless to allow this to go on, but she didn't care, even if she had to pay for it afterwards in heartache. Just this once she wanted to throw caution to the wind. She peeked at him from under her lashes. 'Part of it, I wasn't even born.'

'I'm not that old!' he protested, then sobered a little. 'How do you feel today?'

'Much better, thanks to you,' she answered truthfully. But for him, she wouldn't have slept at all.

'No hangover?'

Surprised, she hadn't thought about it, but there was none of the usual dread. 'No,' she said, smiling with relief.

'That's good,' Aidan murmured, moving so that she shifted on to her back. 'Because I have a confession to make. I would very much like to make love to you, Kate Crawford.'

She gasped. 'W-what? But I thought...'

His finger came up to press against her lips. 'I know you did, but you got the wrong end of the stick.' His voice thickened. 'I want you very much, but yesterday was the wrong time.'

She wasn't stupid. She knew he wasn't saying he loved her. Knew, too, that he would accept her refusal if that was what she wanted. He was leaving it entirely up to her. But she didn't want to refuse. She loved him. For a little while he could be hers. If that was foolish, only she would know. She wasn't going to look further than that.

'Is today the right time?' she whispered huskily.

His fingers lowered to where her pulse throbbed rapidly in her neck. 'I hope so.'

'So do I. Kiss me, Aidan,' she urged with a breathy passion.

A husky laugh broke from him. 'Oh, Kate, that should be——'

He got no further, for her arms went up around his neck and drew his mouth down to hers in a kiss that wiped out any doubts. It was like before, only more piercingly sweet. The fire inside them swiftly broke the bounds of their control. Each kiss was deeper than the last, more sensually arousing. She shivered with pleasure as his hand stroked down to her breast, kneading it until it swelled to fill his palm, and then his lips followed, teasing her nipple through the silky nightdress, driving her wild until with a moan he took her into his mouth, making her cry out with pleasure.

Kate felt molten with desire, her body restless with an ache that demanded appeasement. Her hands glided over the silken skin of his shoulders and back, loving the feel of him, delighting as he shuddered beneath her touch. She longed to feel his flesh against hers without any barrier.

So it was doubly shocking that when Aidan's hand lowered to begin a slow glide up her thigh, she went absolutely rigid, and in a voice filled with loathing, she cried out 'No!'

Aidan's face was as white as hers as he raised his head to look at her. 'Kate?'

Gulping down a wave of panic, she stared at him. 'I can't. I'm sorry, I can't,' she answered in a voice that was thin and tight.

He didn't move, simply took a deep, steadying breath. 'What happened? What did I do?'

She lifted a hand to her forehead. 'I don't know. It just... Your hand... I couldn't go on. I'm sorry,' she whispered, eyes wide with alarm.

Very carefully he moved away from her and sat up. 'Did I hurt you?'

She shook her head. 'No. That's just it. I don't know what happened. Everything was fine—and then it wasn't. I'm sorry,' she said again, feeling absolutely awful.

Aidan let out a puff of breath. 'It's all right. No harm done.'

How must he be feeling? Her own body still ached with frustration. 'I wasn't teasing you. I wouldn't do that,' she apologised, sitting up and drawing her knees

up under her chin. 'I don't know why I froze like that.
I didn't want to.' If he thought she had been playing
tricks, she didn't know what she would do. Damn, why
did everything seem to be against them?

Aidan's arm snaked around her shoulders and drew
her stiff, huddled figure into his side. 'Stop apologising,
Kate.'

'Why is this happening to me?' she questioned in a
small voice.

'I don't know,' Aidan replied seriously. 'I'm not
qualified to make a judgement. You need to talk. I don't
think you can put it off any longer. I want you to see
a... friend of mine.'

Kate went still. A friend? He'd said something like
that before but she hadn't paid much attention. Now a
prickle of alarm ran down her spine. 'What sort of
friend?'

Hearing her caution, he hesitated a moment before
responding. 'A psychologist. You'll——'

Kate didn't wait to hear more but flung herself away
from him in a furious burst of defensive anger. 'Oh, no.
No way am I going to see one of those!' she cried,
standing up quickly.

Startled by her violent reaction, he stood up too.
'Kate——'

'Don't "Kate" me, Aidan,' she cut in tautly. 'I'm not
going and that's final!' Dear lord, that was all she
needed! A psychiatrist! Someone to tell her she was finally going off her trolley—or worse!

Aidan's lips tightened. 'You little fool, it's for your
own good!'

'Why? Because you think I'm crazy, don't you?' she
exploded, nerves as tense as bowstrings.

His hands came to rest on his hips. 'I do not think
you're crazy. That much I do know. What I can't tell

you is what's happening. You want to know, don't you?' he demanded forcefully.

Her chin went up. 'No, I don't!'

'Is that so?' he challenged belligerently, as angry as she was now, eyes narrowing on the pulse that beat rapidly in her throat. 'What are you afraid of? That you'll discover the truth—or I will?'

Her gaze faltered at that. 'I don't know what you mean.'

'No? Then I'll explain. Perhaps you don't want me to discover that what happened just now was only a tease after all,' Aidan expanded softly.

'That's a lie. I told you what happened!'

His brow rose. 'Then there's no reason to be afraid, is there?'

Kate's heart lurched. 'That's blackmail. I might have known a Crawford would resort to those sort of tactics!' she sneered.

Aidan's nostrils flared as he took an angry breath, then visibly she saw the tension drain out of him. 'All right, Kate, you win,' he said tiredly. 'I won't force you to see one.'

She eyed him doubtfully, even as relief made her legs feel wobbly. 'Good.'

A short silence followed as they faced each other across the bed. Finally Aidan grinned.

'You don't seem overjoyed by your victory.'

'I am,' she rejoined swiftly. 'It's just…I am, all right!' she finished as if daring him to make something of her less than enthusiastic reaction.

Aidan inclined his head, then went to the wardrobe to retrieve clean clothes. 'I'm hungry. I'll see you downstairs in ten minutes for breakfast, OK?' Without waiting for her answer, he was gone.

Leaving Kate feeling as if somehow, in winning, she had lost. She knew it had been pure cowardice that had made her react so strongly to his suggestion. She had been scared at the thought of what she might be told. The last thing she wanted was some bespectacled trick-cyclist poking about in her mind.

She shivered, and realised she was still in her skimpy nightdress, and, despite the central heating, the temperature outside was making itself felt. Gathering fresh clothes, she hastened into the bathroom to shower and change.

Twenty minutes later, warmly clad in brushed cotton jeans and a creamy lambswool sweater, she descended the stairs and made her way to the dining-room. The door was slightly ajar, and as she approached it she heard Netta's voice.

'I appreciate how you feel, Aidan, but I think you're making a mistake.'

'But you'll do it for me anyway,' Aidan's voice cajoled confidently.

Netta groaned. 'I need my head examining!' she exclaimed drily.

Kate pushed the door open at that point and found them smiling fondly at each other over the remains of breakfast. They both turned at her entrance.

'Good morning, Kate. How do you feel?' Netta greeted warmly.

Kate returned her friendly smile. 'Much better, thank you. Whatever it is Aidan wants you to do, don't,' she advised, taking an empty seat and glancing across at him with a glint in her eye.

'Oh, I generally make up my own mind about things,' Netta returned with a laugh.

'He's not above blackmail,' Kate added direly.

'I know,' Netta agreed. 'His father's the same. I only give in to it when it's to my own advantage. Now, what can I get you for breakfast? How does fresh coffee and croissants sound?' she offered, rising and collecting the dirty dishes.

'It sounds delicious,' Kate concurred. 'Let me help you with those.' She went round to collect Aidan's plate. As she reached for it, he caught her wrist, making her glance down quickly.

'Are you sure you won't change your mind?' he queried.

Her mouth set. 'Quite sure, thank you. Now, if you wouldn't mind letting me go?'

'Stop pestering the girl, Aidan. Go and take the dogs for a walk or something. Kate's quite safe with me,' Netta ordered as she would a five-year-old.

Although his brows lifted, he didn't argue. 'I know when I'm not wanted,' was all he said before he obediently left the room.

Kate followed Netta into the kitchen with the crockery and helped her stack it in the dishwasher.

'He's a good boy really,' his stepmother declared as she retrieved the croissants from where they had been keeping warm and put them on the table. 'His heart's in the right place. Sit down, Kate, and help yourself, unless you'd rather go in the other room.'

'No, this is fine,' Kate insisted, pulling out a chair. The kitchen was warm and cosy and smelt of fresh bread and coffee. She broke a croissant apart and spooned on some jam.

'You gave us all a scare last night, you know,' Netta observed, setting a cup of coffee at Kate's elbow and sitting down with her own. 'Nightmares can be terrible things. Have you had many?'

'Too many,' Kate responded wryly.

'You poor thing,' the older woman sympathised. 'Are they always the same? I can remember having ones about water when I was young. But that was because my father thought the best way to learn to swim was simply to chuck you in the deep end,' she explained with a laugh.

Kate smiled half-heartedly. 'I only wish mine were like that. They're all different. In the beginning I saw nothing, but felt fear. Now there's more and more detail, and the fear is worse.' She shivered and reached for her coffee, sipping its warmth gratefully.

Netta's expression was concerned. 'No wonder you're frightened. You've no idea what it means?'

'No,' Kate admitted, combing her fingers through her hair, loosening the pins so that soft tendrils escaped. 'Aidan thinks I may have been raped, and I've blocked it out.'

Netta considered that for a moment. 'I suppose it's possible. I wouldn't blame anyone for wanting to forget that! But how do you feel about it?'

'I know it's ridiculous, but I don't *feel* as if that happened to me,' Kate sighed.

Netta stirred her coffee thoughtfully, watching the liquid circling round. 'Then it probably didn't. Yet you've clearly blocked out something pretty traumatic. The mind blanks out something we can't cope with, so that the conscious mind knows nothing. However, the subconscious relives the trauma in dreams.'

Kate listened to the older woman in numb disbelief. From friendly interest and concern, Netta had become all clinically technical. A slow anger started to burn inside her.

'I don't believe it!' she exclaimed, breaking into the flow of words.

Netta's head shot up at once, and met accusing blue eyes. 'Oh, dear,' she said softly.

Kate ground her teeth. 'You're the "friend", aren't you, Netta?' she demanded to know angrily.

The other woman sighed. 'I told him it wouldn't work.'

'O-oh!' Kate fumed, jumping to her feet and pacing away to the window. At the end of the snowy garden she could see Aidan playing with the dogs. 'The rat!'

'A rat, certainly, but a concerned one,' Netta said from behind her. 'He wants to help. He knows you're frightened, but he knows, too, that we can help to overcome that fear. You know, Kate, very often the fear of knowing is worse than the thing itself. You've told me so much, and I think I can help you. Now that you're here, why don't you tell me the rest? I promise that anything you say will go no further. Aidan will know nothing unless you tell him. What do you say?'

Anger warred with a need for understanding as Kate kept her eyes on that distant figure. A sigh left her, and she turned. 'All right.'

Netta gave her an approving smile. 'Good girl. Now, you sit down again and I'll get the coffee-pot. I think we're going to need it.'

An hour later, Kate let herself out of the back door and huddled her coat closer about her. She felt drained after that talk with Netta, but more confident, too. Aidan, damn him, had been right! But that didn't stop her from being furious over the way he had gone about it.

As her feet crunched through the icy snow, the dogs bounded up to meet her and she fended them off with a laugh, their warm breath tickling her rosy cheeks. Over them, she saw Aidan straighten up, hands going into his pockets as he waited for her to approach him. Toe to toe she faced him, finding it incredibly hard to hold on to her anger in the face of his shame-faced grin.

'That was a rotten trick to pull, Crawford,' she snapped, eyes flashing shafts of blue fire.

'If Muhammad wouldn't go to the mountain...' he returned watchfully.

'Rotten, low and underhand!' she added wrathfully.

His lips twitched. 'It worked.'

'That's no excuse. The end doesn't always justify the means, you know!'

'I wanted to help.'

'You were interfering! Damn you, I could hit you for what you did! You had no right!' She stamped her foot and caught one of the dogs who had slumped down beside her. The yelp had her biting her lip in consternation. 'Now look what you've made me do!' she cried, hunkering down to inspect the damage. There wasn't any, but all around there was plenty of snow. A light of devilment entered her eyes.

In a flash she had swept up a double handful, swinging round and up to send it flying into his face. Aidan had no time to move, and the flakes caught him squarely, melting and dripping down his neck.

'Why you little...! OK, you asked for this.' He bent down, and, with a swiftness born of long practice, fashioned a snowball that winged her way in seconds flat, catching her on her chest.

Within minutes a furious battle had been engaged, but it was no contest. Aidan was too good. He caught her twice to her once, and with formidable accuracy. Her anger fled as she gave way to helpless laughter, slipping and sliding, trying to avoid snowballs and dogs who got underfoot and leapt about barking in wild excitement. Finally one caught her in the face and she staggered back, tripped over a darting dog and stretched her length in the snow.

Laughing, Kate brushed the snow from her eyes and looked up into Aidan's face as he came down beside her.

'Still angry with me?' he asked breathlessly, brushing snow from her face and the hair that had escaped and now lay like a halo about her head.

Her heart kicked in her chest. How on earth, she thought helplessly, did anybody stay angry with him when he looked like that? 'No,' she admitted huskily.

'Then I apologise, humbly. I was only thinking of you. Forgive me?'

She had to firm her resolve to say snappily, 'Don't push your luck!'

He responded with a grin. 'What did Netta say?'

Kate raised her brows. 'Haven't you ever heard of the confidentiality of the medical profession?'

'I have, but I'm not asking her, I'm asking you.'

She sighed and held up her hand. 'Help me up.'

Aidan stood at once and pulled her to her feet, and began to brush the snow off her back. There was a garden seat nearby and they sat on that. One of the dogs came and rested its head on her knee and she stroked it idly.

'Well?' Aidan prompted.

'She said the nightmares were my subconscious reliving something I had deliberately blanked out. That somehow you had triggered it off by reminding me of that trauma I could remember—Philip's death.'

'And?'

Kate flickered a glance at him then away again. 'Clearly a man is involved, and the bed. She thinks there's a chance you could be right. Whatever I've blocked out, it's traumatic, and there's nothing more so than rape,' she told him quietly. What she didn't say was that Netta had put forth another possibility. That she had blocked out something *she* had done, and not something that had been done *to* her. The implications of that were even worse than the other, and she would rather keep it to herself.

'She also said I have to be patient, because the memory won't be rushed. She advised me not to fight it, just let it come, and try not to worry.'

'In other words, forget about it as much as you can,' Aidan said thoughtfully.

Kate pulled a face. 'You make it sound easy.' She didn't for a minute think it would be.

'At least we can make it easier. I promised you a sightseeing trip, and that's what we'll do. Keep you too busy to think. What do you say?' he put forward.

'We can try,' she agreed sceptically.

'O, ye of little faith,' Aidan laughed, standing and pulling her up with him. 'Come on, let's get out of these wet clothes before we catch pneumonia, then I'll prove to you how wrong you are.'

Kate allowed herself to be ushered towards the house, not believing for a minute that it would work, but happy to go along with it for the chance to spend time with him in harmony.

As it turned out, Aidan was right. She had very little time to think. They spent that day and those following touring the nation's capital. Aidan was completely relaxed as he gave her a mini history lesson at the Jefferson and Lincoln Memorials. Hand in hand they strolled through the museums and art galleries. With his arm around her shoulder, she stood in driving snow outside the White House, listening to him, uncaring that her feet were freezing and that her nose was bright red.

It was a magical time, and Kate fell more and more deeply in love with him. They went skating by the light of the moon, or took the dogs for long walks, and even went tobogganing on a sled Aidan unearthed from the cellar. Her memories were all of laughter, for by some quirk of fate the nightmares seemed to have stopped.

Everything would have been wonderful, except for one thing. The unexpected realisation that she was in love with Aidan, and the new emotions this awakened in her, had made her forget something vitally important. Never having expected to fall in love, she had never expected to want a man the way she did Aidan. Had never imagined how compelling was the need to have that love consummated. Now, rather late in the day, reality returned.

But for fate, she could even now have been pregnant, for it had never occurred to her to take precautions. It had never seemed necessary. Now the possibility forced her to face facts. To have Aidan's child would have been wonderful, if the marriage had been founded on love and commitment. To bring a child into a marriage pre-destined to fail would be irresponsible. Aidan would make a good father, and he would probably insist on the marriage's continuing if there were a child, but that would only lead to destruction. It was tempting, but the risks were too great, because although she loved him all she knew was that he wanted her. However painful, she had to be sensible, and that left her with only one course to take: to draw back from the brink.

It was hard, but in this she found she had Aidan's help, and it brought her near to tears. For his under-standing was based on a misconception. He thought her physical withdrawal in bed was due to the same reason as before. With a sensitivity that left her humbled, he shrugged off his own frustration, insisting on holding her in his arms, giving her the comfort of untroubled nights, that she knew were a strain for him by the fact that he got very little sleep at all.

When she tried to protest, he told her not to be silly and wouldn't listen to any argument until she was forced to give up. But the guilt gnawed at her. She couldn't understand why he would put himself through that for her. When she found the courage to ask him, he pretended not to hear, leaving her in a state of helpless confusion.

Yet they were, on the whole, happy days, so far removed from the anger of their first meeting that that time seemed like a million years ago.

On Thursday evening Netta and Aidan Senior took them out to dinner in belated celebration of the wedding. Since that long talk with Netta, all hint of reserve had gone, and she and Kate had formed a bond that Kate knew she would sorely miss when this marriage ended, as it was doomed to do. Meanwhile, she had taken to living each day as it came and was storing up memories for the future, while trying hard not to think that the future would not include Aidan.

For tonight she had chosen to wear a simple cocktail dress of lavender jersey with long sleeves and a V-neckline. Netta had decided on a russet-coloured two-piece, while both men looked extremely elegant in white silk shirts and black dinner suits.

A table had been booked at the country club, and consequently there were a lot of introductions to be made and congratulations to receive. Dinner itself was a lively meal, for Aidan's father took it upon himself to acquaint Kate with some of the wilder stories of his son's youth. Aidan took it all in good part, laughing at himself easily, before adding one or two tales that made his father blush.

It had been a long time since Kate had felt part of a family, and it gave her a warm feeling inside to have been accepted so readily by these two genuinely nice people. She was totally unaware of how much she had blossomed in their company, or that more than one significant look was exchanged over her head that night.

Halfway through the evening, when father and son had been called away to help settle an argument, the two women found themselves temporarily abandoned. Netta chose that moment to raise her glass to the younger woman.

'I drink to you, Kate. I'll admit I had reservations about you in the beginning, but I take them all back. You've worked wonders. Aidan isn't the same man these days. It's all due to you. You make him very happy. Life hasn't always been good to him, you know. But I can see you love him, and that's what he needs,' she declared with a smile.

Kate felt choked. 'Thank you, Netta.' Her eyes were drawn to where Aidan and his father stood talking to friends. 'I do love him, very much,' she admitted aloud for the first time.

Netta covered her hand. 'And he loves you.'

Kate smiled and didn't contradict her. 'You've been very generous to me, considering Aidan and I met under very... difficult circumstances. I was so mixed up then, but I'm glad now that I changed my mind and decided to help him. When Andrew told me about the will...' She let the sentence tail off.

'What will was that?' Netta asked, her attention partially caught by a friend at another table.

Kate blinked, frowning at her mother-in-law's distracted smile. 'You know. The one Aidan's grandfather made, cutting him out if he didn't marry,' she explained slowly.

Netta frowned. 'His grandfather? But... Oh!' Slow colour rose in her cheeks. 'Oh, yes, of course, that will.' She laughed nervously. 'You must forgive me, my mind was wandering. Naturally we were all very pleased.'

Kate felt a ball of anger grow in her stomach as she watched Netta gulp at her drink. Her eyes flew to Aidan and narrowed as she saw him laugh. Of all the underhand... 'There was no will, was there?' she demanded to know in a wrathful voice that had quelled many a strong man in its time.

'Well, naturally there was a will, Kate,' Netta argued tensely.

'But no time limit. No threat of losing control of Cranston's!' Her teeth ground together. 'Aidan made it all up, didn't he? He even had you go along with it. Why?'

'Whatever he did or didn't do, he had good reasons for. But I'm afraid if you want to know you'll have to ask him, Kate,' Netta regained her poise.

Kate flashed her a look. 'Don't think I won't! He tricked me. Everything he said was a lie! He didn't need to marry me or anyone! So why pretend he did?'

To Kate's surprise, Netta chuckled. 'An intelligent girl like you ought to be able to work out the answer to that, my dear.'

'What do you mean?' Kate frowned round at her.

'Oh, Kate, it isn't only a female prerogative to feel vulnerable, you know. Think about it. Now smile, they're coming back.'

Kate looked up to find the two men bearing down on them. With an effort she wiped her face clean of anger as Aidan came to her side.

'Dance, Kate?'

Her smile didn't reach her eyes as she gave him her hand and allowed him to lead her on to the dance-floor. This time, when his arms enfolded her, she refused to melt. She was far too angry, and Aidan was far too astute not to pick it up.

'What's the matter, Kate?'

'Nothing. Why should anything be wrong?' she queried, acid-sweet.

She felt his wariness in the stiffening of his body. 'I don't know, but I'd bet a fortune there is.'

Kate's fingers curled into fists on his shoulders. 'The same fortune your grandfather left you in his will? The one you married me for?' she went on dulcetly.

For a moment he didn't speak, and then when he did, there was an odd note in his voice. 'Ah,' he murmured.

This time she looked up, her eyes flashing angrily. 'I'll give you, "ah", you liar!' she breathed furiously.

'Kate, you look magnificent when you're angry,' he told her on a distinctly unsteady note.

She ignored the provocation with an effort. At least he wasn't pretending ignorance. 'Why? Just tell me that. Why?'

'The why ought to be simple, Kate, if you think about it,' he said softly.

'Meaning you aren't going to tell me?'

'I told you once that angry people don't see further than their own anger,' he pointed out, aggravatingly calm.

'I don't need any more potted psychology, thank you very much! If I was as intelligent as both you and Netta seem to imagine, I'd never have married you in the first place!' she declared, aggrieved, and turned her head away, refusing to look at him for the remainder of the dance.

Whether it was the music or some other influence, she didn't know, but gradually her first anger began to die away. At the same time other thoughts started to seep in. The main one was that he hadn't needed to marry her at all, and yet he had tricked her into doing so. It made no sense. Unless... Her heart gave a wild lurch. No. It couldn't be. He couldn't... love her, could he?

It was a notion that sent her thoughts winging in all sorts of crazy directions. Yet the more she probed his motives, the more it seemed to be the only one that made sense. And yet she couldn't accept it. Didn't dare to, lest she be wrong. To have an impossible dream suddenly brought within your grasp was unnerving.

In an agony of uncertainty, she heard the music finish. She looked up at him then, hot colour invading her cheeks as she met his intent grey eyes.

'Aidan?' Her voice was barely more than a whisper.

He smiled. 'That was the last waltz. We'd better join Netta and Dad. With luck we can leave before the crush starts.'

That was all she got out of him until they arrived home nearly three quarters of an hour later, the traffic on the roads being unseasonally heavy. Netta offered to make them all a nightcap when they got in, but Aidan refused, declaring he was tired. So they both said goodnight and made their way upstairs.

They had both been using the en-suite bathroom since that first night. Now Kate watched as Aidan swiftly divested himself of shoes and suit and bagged the shower first, with a grin that made half of her want to hit him, and the other kiss him.

Kate sank on to the bed, kicked off her shoes and scowled after him. He could afford to sound cheery. His world wasn't in utter turmoil. His—— The glum thoughts were cut off abruptly by a startled yelp from the bathroom. Straightening in alarm, Kate stared at the door. What on earth? She was just about to get up and investigate when the door shot open and Aidan reappeared like a bullet.

He stopped when he saw her watching him, half pointed into the room he had left so precipitately, then changed the move into raking a hand through his hair.

The other one was holding on to his only covering—a towel sat at a very rakish, not to say dangerous, angle.

Kate bit her lip on a sudden urge to giggle. She'd never seen him so discomposed. 'Whatever is it?'

Aidan looked from her to the bathroom, then uttered a defeated sigh. 'Oh, hell, what's the use! How are you with spiders, Kate?'

'Spiders? I... Oh!' Now she understood, and her hand came up to hide her smile. 'What would you do if I hated them too?' she asked mockingly.

'Kate!' Her name was ground out in heavy warning.

She rose gracefully. 'All right, where is it, this monster?' she asked wearily, arming herself with a handkerchief he had left on the dresser.

'God, women! It's in the shower. So if you wouldn't mind hustling your butt. We don't have all night,' he gritted out.

She found it where he said—a giant of its kind, less than quarter of an inch from leg, to leg, to leg... She caught it up in the hankie and shook it out of the window. Turning to go back to the bedroom, she was in time to see Aidan's head pop round the door.

'Has it gone?' he demanded.

Kate had to bite down hard on her lip to stop from grinning. She looked him up and down. 'My hero!' she said unsteadily, watching his face darken.

'You're enjoying this, aren't you?'

'How old did you say you were?' she murmured, walking past him.

Aidan took a deep breath. 'Kate Crawford, you're a wretch!'

She couldn't help it, she just couldn't hold the laughter back any longer. 'You should have s-seen your f-face!' she gasped, collapsing on to the bed in gales of laughter. Tears were streaming from her eyes, so she didn't see the way his face changed, eyes dancing with retribution—and something else.

'Funny, was it?' he queried mildly, advancing.

Kate barely noticed as she nodded and wiped her eyes. 'I'm sorry, I'm sorry! I know I shouldn't laugh, but...oh, Aidan, you looked so...so...' Her voice trailed off as he dragged her to her feet.

'That,' he said, dropping a kiss on her startled lips, 'was for laughing. And that——' he did it again, lingering a shade longer '—was because I enjoyed it the first time. And this——' his arms closed about her, lips fastening on hers, demanding a response she couldn't withhold '—this,' he repeated huskily, 'is because I love you, Kate Crawford.'

With a swift peck on her nose, he let her go. Stunned, Kate plopped down on to the bed, and with a grin that flipped her heart over Aidan disappeared into the bathroom.

It took a full minute for the realisation of what he had said to penetrate her brain, but when it did she was galvanised into action. Jumping from the bed, she rushed into the bathroom to yank open the glass door of the shower.

'What did you say?' she demanded breathlessly as the steam slowly evaporated.

Like a snake his arm shot out, encircling her waist, drawing her in under the spray and into his arms. She was soaked in seconds, but she didn't care, blinking up at him as his hands framed her head.

'I said I love you,' he repeated solemnly. One eyebrow rose at her silence. 'Nothing to say?'

Her head shook helplessly. 'Oh, Aidan! I love you too. So much. I thought...'

'You think too much, and all the wrong things. Just shut up and kiss me,' he growled, and brought her head up to his.

It seemed to Kate that as their lips met they exchanged souls, so piercingly sweet was it. An affirmation of something that transcended the purely physical. But then, as always, chemistry took over, and each kiss became deeper as the flames took hold. Gasping, she threw her head back as he rained kisses along her jaw and down the cord of her neck. Eagerly she pressed her body against his, made vitally aware that he was naked and that her sodden dress and tights were scant barrier.

Then they were no barrier at all as Aidan slid down the zip and peeled them away from her, and she moaned her pleasure as flesh met flesh. Delicious thrills chased each other along her spine as the hairs on his chest teased her aching breasts, and she arched herself closer, trying to ease their need. The feel of his hands caressing and moulding her was electrifying and with a groan she pressed her lips to his shoulder, tasting him with her tongue. His hands dropped to her buttocks, bringing her dizzily up against him and unconsciously her nails dug into the flesh of his back.

Aidan gasped, head raising from its plundering of her nape. 'Hey, little cat, that smarts!' he growled with a laugh.

But Kate wasn't laughing. Her body froze, jack-knifing away from him. She backed away, arms crossing protectively over her breasts. 'Don't call me that!' she cried, the words tearing from a painfully tight throat.

Aidan had taken a step towards her, but now he stopped, hands clenching into fists at his sides as he strove for control. Slowly he reached out and turned off the water. The silence that fell throbbed with their seething emotions. Kate turned away, unable to bear the grim tautness of his face. She heard the door click open, then the fluffy folds of a towel were draped about her shoulders. Slowly she turned, tucking in the ends. Aidan had draped a towel about his hips, and her eyes rose upwards, over a chest that heaved as he steadied his breathing, then sought his face.

She ran a hand over her brow. 'I'm sorry. It was that name. He called me that. I can't bear it!'

Aidan's hand came out to run caressingly up and down her arms. 'What am I going to do with you?' he sighed.

Tears sprung to her eyes. 'Oh, God, Aidan! How can you love me when I do this to you?'

He drew her in to his chest, chin resting on her hair. 'I'm just crazy, I guess. Crazy in love with you.'

She closed her eyes. 'It isn't fair!'

'It won't always be like this, you know.'

'How can you be so sure?' she whispered.

'Because we love each other. We'll work it out. When you hear me complaining, that's the time to worry. Come on, let's get to bed. It's late and we're both tired.' He disappeared into the other room.

Kate dried herself, then rubbed her hair until it was only barely damp before returning to the bedroom to slip into a clean nightdress. Aidan was already in bed. He watched as she went to the dressing-table and picked up her brush, beginning to run it through her hair.

'Come over here and let me do that,' he commanded gently, and, with only the slightest hesitation, she did, sitting down on the edge of the bed, while Aidan rose on to his knees behind her and started to brush her hair.

Kate closed her eyes as the rhythmic strokes drained the last of the tension out of her. The silence was punctuated only by the sound of their breathing. They could have been alone on a desert island. A sigh escaped her.

'How could you love me? I was so awful when we met,' she said huskily.

There was a smile in his voice as he answered. 'I asked myself the same question. I came there to make you feel guilty and, to my surprise, I found myself saying and doing something completely different. The simple fact was that I saw you holding that little girl, and from that moment on I was lost.'

She was surprised. That long? He'd loved her that long? 'Truly?'

'Truly,' he repeated wryly. 'When I realised, I thought I'd been as foolish as all those other men, and I was determined not to let you know. Demanding that you marry me was an inspired moment—a moment of lunacy, I sometimes thought. Yet I wanted to have you. To be the only man in your life. Andrew's mix-up over the will gave me just the excuse I needed.'

'Then why were you marrying what's-her-name?' she wanted to know.

'Julia? The truth is I never expected to fall in love, yet I wanted a family. The time seemed right, and Julia was someone I'd known for a long time and liked and respected. But then I met you, and there was nobody else for me. When you turned me down, I went away thinking what an idiot I was, and that your refusal was probably the best thing all round. Yet I couldn't get you out of my mind all that week. I don't know if I'd have tried to contact you again or not, but then your call came. I was intrigued, and if I'm honest, I was relieved that you'd given me the excuse I needed.'

Kate grimaced. 'Andrew's lie.'

'Andrew didn't lie. He believed it. To him it was the truth. He never could see beyond his own hatred. He wanted me to lose everything, so what he overheard was never doubted. And if anyone had tried to convince him otherwise, he would only have believed it more. There's no reasoning with him.

'For once his blindness worked in my favour. You called me, and I was well and truly caught,' he told her simply.

Kate sighed. 'But I was so horrid to you!' she exclaimed remorsefully.

'No more than I was to you. I said things I regret, simply because I was vulnerable. To my mind I'd fallen for you despite all I knew of you and against my own better judgement. I had no plan other than to survive from day to day, but almost from the day we met I realised you weren't at all the way you seemed. That gave me hope that one day I could make you love me.'

A large lump formed in her throat and she had to swallow twice to remove it. 'I didn't know. I thought I hated you, but I was never indifferent. No man had got to me the way you did. You scared me. Perhaps I loved you long before I realised. When I knew, I didn't think you could feel anything for me. I was sure you must hate me, because I'd been every bit as bad as you thought I was,' she confessed.

'I soon discovered it wasn't wise to take you at face value. I found you were quite a different person. Vulnerable in ways I wouldn't have believed from your reputation. I could see you needed help, but you fought me. You fought everything. I just held on to the fact that a woman who loves children couldn't be all bad. I'm glad you like them, for I do too.'

Kate caught her breath. Reaching up, she took the brush from him, holding it before her like some kind of shield. 'You want a family?'

His gentle hands kneaded her shoulders. 'A large one. Four at least. How about you?'

She closed her eyes. Their dreams were the same. It would have made everything perfect, except for one thing. She licked dry lips. 'I always wanted a family, too. But what if we can never have them? What if——?'

He drew her into his arms, cutting off her hesitant words. 'Sweetheart, I refuse to think in terms of never. If I did that, I'd never have married you and never discovered you love me.'

Kate twisted round, her face pressing into his neck as she fought back tears. 'Oh, Aidan, I love you. So very, very much,' she breathed against his skin.

His lips brushed her hair. 'That's all I want to know. Let the future take care of itself. Believe me, we're going to be very, very happy. This is where you belong, Kate. This is where you stay.'

'Well?' Netta asked, when Kate joined her in the kitchen for breakfast next day. 'Did you work it out?'

To Kate's dismay a fiery blush worked its way up her neck and into her cheeks. Still she joined in when Netta laughed. 'Yes, I did. I must have been blind.'

Netta shook her head. 'That makes two of you. You won't believe the conversations I've had with Aidan over you. Still, all's well that ends well. It's the perfect birthday present for him.'

Kate's jaw dropped; she'd completely forgotten. 'Birthday? It can't be!'

Netta pointed to the big red cross marked on the calendar. 'It is. Tomorrow. He'll be thirty-eight.'

'But I don't have anything!' Kate exclaimed feeling absolutely dreadful.

'Don't panic,' Netta advised. 'I'm going into town today. You can come with me and pick something up. You're bound to find something.'

Netta was right. She found just the thing in a tiny antique shop. It was a small jade carving of a sleeping tiger, and she knew instinctively that he would appreciate it.

She gave it to him over a candlelit dinner the following evening. Netta had suggested the restaurant, and the setting was as romantic as Kate could have wished. He unwrapped the gift carefully, and when he finally held it in his hand, his eyes told her what words couldn't. He raised his glass of champagne to her in a toast.

'You are the most incredibly beautiful woman. Remind me to thank you properly for my present later,' he declared softly, reaching out for her hand.

'I will,' she smiled back, all her love in the dazzling blue of her eyes.

'Then here's to you, my own sleeping tigress. To you and the future.'

In the low lighting, he didn't see the way her colour faded. 'I'll drink to that.' She raised her glass to her lips briefly, then added fervently, 'I'm going to make sure you never have to regret marrying me.'

'That I could never do,' he assured her, eyes holding hers.

Kate smiled, but a shiver ran through her, as if someone had just walked over her grave. Though she tried to shake it off, for the rest of the evening she had a dreadful presentiment of looming disaster.

It was late when they drove home, but the lights were still on, and there was the sound of voices coming from the lounge. Curiosity drew them to the open doorway. It was Netta who saw them first, and she came to her feet in a movement devoid of her usual grace.

'Well, here you are at last. You'll never guess who's turned up, Aidan,' she declared edgily, eyes shooting to the end of the room.

Automatically they followed her gaze. Both froze as a lazy figure rose from his chair.

'I've come to wish you a happy birthday, brother,' Andrew Crawford drawled into the silence that fell.

CHAPTER NINE

INSTINCTIVELY Kate moved closer to Aidan, feeling again that flood of anxiety she had experienced when last she had faced his brother. Aidan's arm fastened about her waist, and she could feel the tension in him. Though he looked relaxed, his whole body was braced for this unexpected meeting.

'Well? Aren't you going to say anything? Or do you intend to stand in the doorway forever?' Andrew taunted mockingly.

'What do you want, Andrew?' Aidan asked warily, refusing to rise to the bait. Kate could sense his reluctance for this exchange as he urged her into the room ahead of him.

Andrew laughed, 'I've already told you. I've no excuse for forgetting your birthday, have I?'

Aidan's free hand was extended. 'And I've no reason to believe anything is ever that simple with you. But I'll call your bluff. Happy birthday.'

They shook hands, Andrew's smile the epitome of brotherly affection, his twin's ruefully watchful.

'You've met my wife, Kate,' Aidan said by way of introduction, and for the first time she felt the impact of Andrew's gaze.

His lips curved reminiscently, but his eyes were cold. 'Ah, yes, Kate. Netta did happen to mention you'd acquired a lovely young bride. I hadn't expected it to be Kate, but the world is full of surprises. As I recall, our last meeting had rather a dampening effect.' Though light, his voice carried an edge nobody missed.

Kate met Aidan's querying glance and explained. 'I threw a glass of water over him,' she said, not bothering to hide her satisfaction.

'She always was impulsive,' Andrew drawled smoothly.

Netta, who had remained silently watching up till now, spoke up. 'If you three intend to talk over old times, I'll leave you to it. Your father went up ages ago, and I need my beauty sleep these days. Andrew, you'll have your usual room, of course. I'll see you all in the morning. Goodnight.'

With her departure, there was a subtle change in the atmosphere. That sense of impending disaster returned to Kate, tensing her muscles as she watched the two brothers confronting each other.

'So,' Andrew said conversationally. 'You kept control of the company. How noble of Kate to step into the breach.'

'The company was never in doubt, Andrew. You should have made sure of your facts before you started spreading rumours. Whatever our personal differences, Grandfather would never have left the controlling interest anywhere but in the family,' Aidan told him softly.

Chagrin darkened his twin's face. 'You always did have the devil's own luck, brother!'

'I was certainly lucky to marry Kate.'

'And how well the marriage has turned out. Netta tells me she's never seen two people more in love than you.'

Kate felt Aidan's arm tighten, and she glanced up, smiling. 'We're very happy,' she confirmed huskily. Looking back at Andrew, her eyes dared him to deny it.

He held up his hands. 'I'm pleased for you. I really am.' A slow smile crossed his handsome face. 'It's strange how things work out. One moment you can be in the depths of gloom, and the next a whole world of possibilities open up. Not having realised you were married, I had nothing to give you, and that upset me. But now I know just the present. I think a toast is in order. You do the honours, Aidan. I'll have Scotch on the rocks.'

'I don't suppose this can wait until tomorrow?' Aidan suggested pointedly.

'Certainly not. It wouldn't be your birthday,' Andrew insisted.

Releasing her, Aidan gave Kate a bracing smile and crossed over to the cocktail cabinet. Andrew watched him for a second, then turned to smile at Kate. She stiffened her spine automatically, chin lifting defiantly.

'I hope Kate's been treating you well.' He spoke to his brother without taking his eyes off her. 'I'd hate to think that all my efforts have been wasted, and that you're disappointed. To look at her, you wouldn't imagine how wild she can be,' he mused.

Kate gasped, her eyes flying from Andrew to Aidan, who had stopped what he was doing and had turned, his body set rigid.

'Just what are you trying to say, Andrew?' he demanded tightly.

His brother ignored him, moving instead to stand before Kate, his hand reaching up to caress her cheek, smiling as she flinched away. 'Well, little cat, are you still using your claws?'

At the sound of that hated name, the world seemed to tilt beneath Kate's feet. Something struck her in the chest like a thunderbolt, stealing her breath and all the blood drained from her face, leaving her white and shaken.

Her, 'No!' clashed with Aidan's,

'My God!'

Malice glittered in his grey eyes as Andrew surveyed the tableau of stricken figures. 'Oh, dear, didn't Kate tell you I'd already had her?' he mocked.

With a groan, Kate's hands flew to her cheeks. She flinched at the sound of crashing glass as Aidan slammed a bottle down and closed the space between himself and his brother in two angry strides. There was murder in his eyes as he roughly spun Andrew round.

'You? It was *you* who raped her?' The words were forced out through a barrier of murderous rage.

Andrew's brows rose. 'Rape?' he queried with a laugh. 'Is that what she told you? Oh, no, I didn't use force, I didn't need to. She went to bed with me for money, my dear brother, and believe me, she was worth every penny!'

Aidan's head went back as if from a blow. He, too, was pale now. 'I don't believe you.'

'Then ask her, dear boy, and see if she dares deny it,' his brother riposted and they both turned towards her.

Shaking like an aspen, Kate felt the accusation of their eyes like a blow. Nausea rose to choke her. She couldn't speak, didn't even see them, only the pictures, no longer blocked, that flashed before her mind's eye. At last everything was revealed to her, and with a strangled moan of self-disgust she turned and fled from the room.

Hall, stairs and landing were just stages in her flight. Her goal was their room, and, once there, she sank down on the side of the bed, body rocking as she bore the pain, arms clamped around her waist.

She knew now, knew it all, and she could no longer hide from the truth. Now she knew why she had feared Andrew, for he alone had known the truth. She had done exactly what he had said, and all the loathing and self-disgust swelled the ball of sickness in her stomach.

She jumped violently as the door clicked open, head shooting round. Aidan stood there watching her, his face so coldly set that he was like a stranger, not the man she had grown to love at all. Dumbly she watched as he shut the door and prowled towards her. He stopped only inches away and she winced as his hand tipped her head up until her neck ached and she couldn't avoid his gaze.

'Tell me it isn't true,' he demanded through his teeth. 'Tell me you didn't sleep with my own brother for money.'

Pain darkened her eyes, and she tried to look away, but he jerked her back roughly.

'Tell me, damn you!'

She swallowed, eyes pleading for understanding. 'I...can't,' she croaked, and gasped as he thrust her backwards so that she sprawled on the bed. The angry force of his body followed her down, pinning her beneath him.

There was a wildness in his eyes she had never seen before as he stared down at her. 'Money? Is that where I've gone wrong, Kate? Should I have offered you money to sleep with me?' he bit out in an emotion-filled voice.

Her eyes burned. He was so hurt! She could feel his pain as if it were her own. 'Aidan, don't,' she begged brokenly, trying to escape.

He pushed her back. 'How much, Kate?'

She saw him through a veil of tears. 'You don't understand!'

'Don't I? Don't I? All I understand right now is that you've been driving me crazy, walking on eggshells round you because I believed, God help me, you'd been raped. Now I find it's all a lie and that my own brother... God damn you, Kate! Just name your price, but now I'm taking something on account!'

His mouth ground down on hers with the full force of his anger. Sobbing wildly, she tried to avoid him, but he was too strong, too angry and betrayed. She felt the tearing of the soft skin of her lips and tasted blood, and the nausea rose to her throat. With a strength she didn't know she had, she threw out a hand and caught him a blow on the side of the head. It weakened his hold just enough for her to roll from beneath him. Tumbling from the bed, she staggered to the bathroom.

She was only just in time, sinking to her knees to be violently sick. How long it lasted, she didn't know, but finally there was nothing left, and she dropped her head on her hands, shivering with cold. She only realised Aidan was beside her when the toilet flushed, then gentle hands that shook ever so slightly, raised her to sit on the edge of the bath and a cold flannel was wiped over her face.

Only when it stopped did she look up at him. The wildness was gone from his eyes, replaced now by a mixture of remorse and concern.

'Kate, I'm sorry,' he apologised huskily. 'I don't know what came over me.'

She looked away, swallowing painfully. 'Don't you?' she demanded tautly, forcing herself to meet his eyes again. 'What else did he say to you, Aidan? That I enjoyed it too? That I couldn't get enough?' The set of his face told her she was right. 'Don't you know that my flesh crawls at the thought that I could ever have let him touch me? You don't know what it cost me to do that!' Tears flooded her eyes, but she held them back somehow. 'I sank my pride and abandoned my self-respect because I was desperate! Oh, God!' she shuddered with revulsion. 'I feel so dirty. So ashamed.'

White-faced, Aidan's throat worked madly to clear a constriction. 'Andrew did this to you...in my name?' he questioned thickly.

Kate shivered. 'I don't want to talk about it.'

'You have to. For your own sake it must come out in the open,' he declared firmly. 'And I have to know everything,' he finished on a grim note.

She knew he was right, however reluctant she was to relive that time in her life. 'Very well,' she agreed in a dull voice, 'but not here.'

She led the way back into the bedroom. The sight of the rumpled bed made her wince, and she avoided it, going instead to the small couch set under the window. She curled up in one corner, arms hugging her knees, lids lowered to shield her eyes. Following her, Aidan perched on a corner of the bed, elbows on knees, hands loosely clasped, belying the tension in him.

Kate drew in a shaky breath, marshalling her thoughts. 'You remember I told you I came to ask you for help for Philip? You never did ask me why. Philip had been ill for some time. The disease was a rare one. Little was known about it, but there was a treatment available that offered a good chance of recovery. But it would mean going to America, and, worse, the cost of the treatment itself was enormous. I didn't earn the sort of money I needed. I was at the end of my tether when I remembered my father had once told me to go to Aidan Crawford if ever I was in trouble. Of course, I'd never met him, but I had no qualms about going to see him. Besides, I was desperate—Philip was getting worse by the hour, it seemed to me. I allowed myself to hope because that was all I had left. And so I went to see him . . .'

Aidan Crawford's house was in one of those quiet, elegant little squares that had the unmistakable atmosphere of understated affluence. A dark-suited man-servant opened the door to her summons and enquired her business.

'I would like to see Mr Crawford,' she said as authoritatively as she could. Accurately guessing that his function was to shield his employer from unwanted visitors, she quickly added, 'It's a private matter, and extremely urgent.'

The man looked sympathetically regretful. 'I'm afraid——' he began but got no further.

'Show her in, Bates, there's a good fellow,' a voice commanded from somewhere inside.

A flicker of annoyance passed over the man Bates's face, but he stepped back none the less. 'Very good, sir. If you would care to step inside, miss,' he invited smoothly.

Kate found herself shown into what was clearly the study. Aidan Crawford was standing by the fireplace. He was a big, handsome man, a little younger than she'd expected, and when he smiled at her she quickly noticed that it didn't reach his eyes. They were calculatingly assessing as they roved over her from head to toe. She wasn't used to being stared at this way, and she shivered, the hairs on the back of her neck rising atavistically.

If her mission hadn't been so imperative, she would have turned and walked away as quickly as her legs could carry her, but, whatever her feelings, this man had been her father's friend and she needed his help. So she went forward and shook the hand he held out to her, disliking the possessive way he held on to hers just a fraction too long.

'You wanted to speak to me? In what way can I help you, Miss...?' he paused significantly.

'Taylor-Hardie,' Kate supplied, using her full name to jog his memory, though she rarely used it herself. 'Kate Taylor-Hardie. Yes, I did want to speak to you. We've never met, but you did know my father, Christopher Taylor-Hardie.'

Aidan Crawford rubbed his chin thoughtfully. 'Ah, yes, Christopher.' He moved round behind her as he spoke and his hands came to rest on her shoulders. 'Naturally I'm delighted to meet any relative of his. Let me take your coat.' He relieved her of it before she could protest. 'Now, do sit down, and tell me how I may help you.'

Kate seated herself on a chair facing the desk as he took his seat behind it. 'Actually, I'm here on my brother's behalf. Philip is . . . Philip . . .' She hesitated at the brink, not quite knowing how to phrase her request now the moment had arrived. She was saved the trouble.

'Kate . . . I may call you that, I hope, as a friend of the family? Kate, Philip's in trouble, isn't he? Why don't you tell me all about it?' he invited confidentially.

Mightily relieved, she did just that. At the end of the tale, he sat back in his chair, eyes assessing her once more.

'How much do you need?' he asked finally, and she stated a figure that caught her breath but didn't so much as make him blink. He was so calm, she began to hope her plea hadn't been made in vain. 'That's a lot of money.'

She bit her lip. 'I know, but I can assure you that every penny will be paid back,' she hastened to add.

After a long pause, Aidan Crawford rose to his feet and took a pensive turn about the room. Kate followed him with her eyes as far as she could, until he disappeared behind her. It came as an unwelcome shock when his hands came to rest on her shoulders again, pressing down in a sort of massaging action.

'You know, Kate,' he murmured, 'you're asking a lot from friendship. I'm not running a benevolent society, you know. However, I can't help thinking there's a way for a young woman like you—a very beautiful woman, I might add—to make the risk worth my while.'

Kate very nearly choked, scarcely able to credit what she was hearing. She wasn't green. She knew what he was suggesting, and it was unbelievable. It was like something out of a Victorian melodrama.

'What?' The incredulous question was forced from her. How could this man, her father's friend, be saying such a thing?

Aidan Crawford laughed way down deep in his throat. 'Come now, you're not unintelligent.' His hands began to caress up and down her arms.

She repressed a shudder of intense disgust, her attempt to stand foiled by remarkably strong hands. 'I thought you were a friend!' she exclaimed angrily.

'Oh, I am, but you can't expect me to do this for nothing. If I'm to be generous, surely you can be generous too.'

The idea was sickening. 'You must be mad if you think I'd agree to anything so disgusting!' she uttered in violent refusal.

He bent down so that his mouth was close to her ear. 'It seems a reasonable bargain. One you are, of course, entirely free to refuse. But don't I remember you telling me you'd come here as a last resort? So it seems to me that your answer depends on just how much you love your brother.'

And there he had her. She had nowhere else to go. It was either do as he suggested, or see her brother deteriorate before her eyes. She loved him too much to do that, so she had no choice.

'You're despicable! How can you call yourself a friend?' she choked.

'Is that a yes or a no, Kate?'

'You know it's yes,' she muttered thickly. 'If you give me the money, I promise to...meet you whenever you say.'

The hands on her arms urged her upwards and turned her to face him. 'Oh, no. The money comes afterwards, Kate. Of course I trust you, but people can be forgetful. So, we have a deal,' he declared with satisfaction. 'All the best bargains are sealed with a kiss,' he added, and brought his head down.

If she hadn't given her word, she would have run like mad. Honour kept her there although the lips that claimed hers so greedily made her flesh crawl, especially when his tongue insinuated its way between her teeth. Revolted, she only prayed she could bear it as long as necessary.

Although she hadn't responded, he seemed satisfied when he released her. 'I think we'll be more comfortable upstairs, don't you?' he suggested throatily.

There was nothing else for her to do except allow him to lead her back to the hall, and the stairway that led upwards into darkness. Coldness invaded her as she mounted them by his side, feeling as if she was going to her own execution. But she didn't falter, just kept on going, blanking her mind of all thought except that she was doing this for Philip.

What took place behind the closed door of his bedroom was a nightmare. She refused to relax or respond, giving him no encouragement, but she was unable to detach her mind from what happened to her body. He wasn't brutal, just uncaring of her unresponsiveness or her innocence. Calling her his 'little cat', he was not satisfied until long into the night, and by then she was no longer innocent in mind or body. She felt degraded—sullied by a lust that sought pleasure and didn't care if it gave none in return.

Worse, though, followed.

He watched her as she slid from the bed to dress, and when she turned to him and asked for the money, he laughed in her face. 'Did you seriously think I would hand over that sort of money for the pleasure of your body, delectable though it was?' He lay there against the pillows, sheet pulled negligently across his hips, and informed her just how ridiculously naïve he found her. 'I wouldn't give it to you, even if I could, little cat.'

If she had had a knife in that moment, she would have driven it into his lying heart. 'You're beneath contempt! If it's the last thing I do, I'll make you sorry for this, Aidan Crawford!' she swore in bitterness and hatred . . .

Kate came back to the present to find her cheeks wet with tears. She wiped them away with fingers that shook. 'He just lay there and laughed at me,' she added in a painful whisper. 'He just laughed.'

In the silence that fell, she waited for Aidan's response, but none came. She looked at him anxiously. Did he believe her? She couldn't tell. His head was lowered, but his hands were curled into fists on his knees. As if feeling her eyes on him, his head came up, and she breathed in sharply at the pain and anger in his face.

'Oh, Kate, what can I say? Sorry is too bloody inadequate! When I think . . .' He halted abruptly, swallowing, then jumped to his feet and paced away to the dresser. The tension in him was awesome as he crashed his fist against the top. 'This time, by God, he's gone too far!' he declared through gritted teeth, then suddenly he headed for the door.

Eyes wide, Kate swung her legs to the floor. 'Where are you going?'

He didn't miss his step. 'To find my brother and do something I should have done a long time ago!' he flung over his shoulder, and disappeared out into the passage.

Kate's heart thumped wildly as she followed him. At the door she heard his descent of the stairs, and by the time she reached them she could hear angry voices coming from below. She froze then, one foot hovering

on the top step. Then there was a startled yell and the
sound of furniture breaking followed by a sudden silence.
Her hand flew to her lips as she watched Aidan appear
in the hall, one hand massaging the other.

She must have made some noise, for he looked up
sharply. The look on his face was one of grim satisfaction. Slowly he mounted the stairs towards her,
stopping when they were level.

'Andrew has decided not to stay after all,' he said drily.

Reeling a little, Kate's eyes dropped to his hand. She
took it between hers, thumb rubbing softly over bruised
knuckles. 'Then you did believe me?'

His free hand came out to draw her close. 'Oh, yes.
Can you ever forgive us for what you went through?'

'Can you forgive me?' she countered, voice muffled
by his shoulder. Beneath her cheek his chest heaved.

'You have nothing to reproach yourself for, Kate.
There's nothing to forgive.' He eased away a little to
gaze down at her. 'I wish there were something I could
do to wipe away the past completely,' he sighed.

Kate shivered. 'I just want to forget. To put it behind
me once and for all.'

He stared at her, a strange expression in his eyes. 'Can
you, Kate?' he asked gently.

A little shaken, she thought she understood. 'I...don't
know,' she said honestly.

With a wry smile Aidan turned her about and, still
with his arm around her, urged her back to their room.
Kate's eye fell on the bed immediately and she went
across to smooth it out and turn the covers back. Aidan
watched her in silence for a moment then with a sigh he
went to collect his robe from the chair.

'I think we both need some sleep before we make any
decisions,' he offered evenly.

It was the lack of tone that made Kate look up with a frown. 'Do we have any decisions to make?' she questioned, surprised.

'I think so. That's why I intend to sleep in the spare room tonight.'

The statement fell into the pool of silence and sent ripples through the room, and Kate. She tensed.

'You don't have to.'

Aidan half smiled. 'Oh, but I do. Don't worry, I won't be far away if you need me. But I very much doubt you'll be having the nightmares any more. So, sleep well, Kate, and I'll see you in the morning.'

Before she could even start to find the words to argue, he was gone, shutting the door softly behind him. Slowly she sank down on the bed, eyes still on the door. Why had he done that? Why had he gone? A horrible idea came to her. He had said she need not blame herself, but perhaps he couldn't stomach the thought of her with his brother. Had his kindness hidden a disgust of her now?

Painful fingers tightened about her heart. That had to be it. What other explanation could there be? She felt crushed, for how could she fight that? Yet she must, because she loved him too much to allow Andrew to come between them any more. But what to do? What to do?

The question battered her mind long after she had changed and climbed into bed. But it was hard to think when the bed felt cold and empty without Aidan beside her. Finally, in desperation, she reached for his pillow, dragging it into her arms and holding it tight. His scent lingered there, and she squeezed her eyes to hold back foolish tears and buried her face in it.

Eventually she fell asleep like that, heart aching and no nearer a solution than before.

CHAPTER TEN

KATE stood at the kitchen window, a steaming mug of coffee clasped in her hands. She felt chilled, although the room was warm. Nor was it the snow gently falling beyond the glass that made her shiver. It was the man slowly making his way up to the house. There was a set to his shoulders that made her heart contract.

It was early still. They were the only two abroad this early on Sunday morning. She had been awake when Aidan had crept into their room an hour ago to retrieve fresh clothes. But he had made no attempt to approach the bed, so she had remained silent. He hadn't wanted to talk, that was obvious, but his silence after the events last night had driven her to the bedroom window when she'd heard him leave the house, then to dress in jeans and sweater and come down here to wait for him to return.

As he approached the door, she moved back to the table, somehow needing its solid support. Aidan came in, stamping his feet on the mat and shaking the snow from his hair. He was oblivious to her presence until he turned and saw her standing silently watching, the mug still held defensively before her. For an instant a flame burned in his eyes, but then was swiftly dampened. Turning away, he unzipped his coat and shrugged out of it, hanging it on a hook behind the door.

'Boy, it's cold out there!' he declared, rubbing his hands and blowing on them.

'There's fresh coffee in the pot,' Kate offered, putting her mug down, intending to pour him some.

176

'Thanks, I'll get it,' he countered smoothly, crossing to collect a mug and fill it. 'You're up early,' he observed over his shoulder.

'So are you,' she pointed out, hating the way they were sounding like strangers talking to fill an uncomfortable silence.

'I guess neither of us could sleep.' Aidan shrugged, and leant his weight against the counter, sipping appreciatively.

She wished she could just cross the floor and go into his arms, but something held her back. Licking her lips in a purely nervous gesture, she sat down. 'Did you enjoy your walk?'

Aidan looked up from a brooding contemplation of his mug and met her eyes squarely. 'It wasn't that sort of walk.'

She'd known that. It was the reason a ball of ice seemed to be forming in her stomach. Last night she had sensed something was wrong. Daylight had only served to intensify the feeling. He seemed so far away, on the other side of a wall that was shutting her out. She thought she knew why, but she had to know for certain.

'You said we shouldn't make any hasty decisions, but I think you've already made up your mind, haven't you?'

With a sigh, Aidan set his mug aside. 'You're right, of course. There's no easy way to say this, so I'll just have to be blunt. I think we should get a divorce, Kate,' he said evenly.

Kate's heart jerked as painful fingers seemed to tighten about it. Oh, God, she was right! 'You're disgusted, aren't you? Whatever you said, what I did disgusts you, doesn't it?' she demanded in a voice that echoed her pain.

He paled and pushed himself upright, taking a half-step towards her before halting abruptly. 'No!' he said forcefully. 'That's not the reason.'

She dragged her fingers through the cloud of silver hair she had left free about her shoulders. 'I don't believe you! What other reason could there be for you to do this? God knows, I disgust myself, so why shouldn't you feel the same?' she muttered thickly.

Aidan was by her side in an instant, hands reaching out to jerk her to her feet. 'Because I don't! I'm telling you the truth, damn it!'

Kate's eyes were molten sapphire. 'Then why?' she questioned in a voice that broke.

He let her go, hands spreading out in a gesture of helplessness. 'Because I think it's for the best,' he declared hoarsely.

'And if I think it's for the worst?'

His face closed down. 'It makes no difference. Our marriage is doomed to fail, Kate. I can see that, and so should you. The best thing for both of us is to end it now.' He looked at her stricken face and swallowed hard. 'Believe me, it's for the best,' he repeated tersely, and walked swiftly from the room.

Sinking down on to the chair again, she stared after him. She felt numb at the way he had so cold-bloodedly killed off everything that was between them. He had said he loved her, he had been so patient and kind, so why this, now? He had said it wasn't because he was disgusted, and yet he knew their marriage was doomed. What did he mean?

Everything had seemed so perfect. Even when she had intimated her fears that they might never have a normal marriage and children of their own.

With a faint gasp, Kate sat up straighter. Was that it? He had told her that that aspect of their life wasn't a problem, but had he come to realise that he couldn't live with it? Had he found that he couldn't take the knowledge that he might never have the children he longed for?

It was the only possible explanation for his change of heart, and one she couldn't argue with. She loved him, and to wish on him a life that would never feel complete was unfair. Under those circumstances, wasn't the kindest thing to break the knot that tied them? He was right. Better this pain now than that which would surely come.

But it hurt so. A future without him seemed bleak and hopeless. Yet she had to face it with as much self-possession as she could. The sooner she left, the better it would be for both of them. She had the perfect excuse. No one would be surprised that she had to return to England, for her business was there. It would be simple enough then to make whatever excuses necessary for the breakdown of their marriage. A clean break was the only way for them now.

The swish of the door made her look up swiftly, heart thudding in her chest in case it should be Aidan, but it wasn't. It was a house-coated Netta who bustled in, eyebrows lifting in surprise when she saw the younger woman.

'Good morning, Kate, you're up early. What brought this on? I met Aidan fully dressed on the stairs, and when I looked in on Andrew a minute or two ago he wasn't anywhere to be seen either!'

Kate hastily composed her face, not wanting Netta to witness her distress and question it. 'Andrew decided not to stay after all,' she explained.

'Good heavens, that's not like him. Andrew loves his creature comforts. To go out in sub-zero temperatures just isn't his style.'

'Aidan persuaded him,' Kate added drily and gained Netta's complete attention.

'Aidan did? Well, well, well. I take it that accounts for the sudden disappearance of my aspidistra?' Netta declared as she came and sat down opposite Kate. 'Not that I mind. I never liked it, but it was a gift from my aunt, and as she still visits I had to keep it on show. So, tell me what happened?' she urged, all agog.

It was impossible to say nothing, so Kate simply said, 'They had an argument.'

'And Aidan hit him? Well, Andrew's had that coming a long time. I'm glad Aidan finally lost his temper with him. It did neither of them any good for him to act as if his brother could do nothing wrong. Oh, it's too late to save Andrew, but at least he should understand that certain behaviour is unacceptable, even at his age.

'The problem is that Andrew was terribly spoiled by his mother. Everything he wanted, he got, and yet he has this jealous belief that Aidan was the one who had everything. Whereas Aidan never asked for much and would have willingly shared what he had. Sometimes it's hard to think of them as twins,' Netta finished with a shake of her head.

'I know what you mean,' Kate agreed. 'They look alike, and yet their personalities are so different.'

'But though we know their differences, other people don't,' Netta pointed out, warming to what was obviously a pet theme. 'From the outside, if it weren't for Aidan's scar, they could be the same. What do other people see? When they look at one, do they see the other? Do they see differences, or are the boys inter-changeable? Do things you attribute to one automatically transfer to the other? And what of the boys? They know they're different, but everyone looks at them as if they were the same. How galling is it never to be seen as an individual, to always know you're a reminder of the other one?'

Kate's nerves gave an almighty jolt. Netta's last words seemed to echo in her mind, gaining strength. 'To always know you're a reminder of the other one.' Incredible as it might seem, Kate knew she had finally seen the light. The candle of hope that had guttered suddenly flared back into brilliance. All her assumptions had been wrong, and she was going to prove it.

Her sudden jump to her feet startled Netta who had still been talking. The words tailed off as Kate rounded the table to bend and give her an affectionate hug.

'Netta, you're a lifesaver,' she declared huskily.

'I am? I mean, am I?' the older woman queried in bemusement.

Kate laughed, a cheerful, happy sound, full of confidence. 'Yes, and don't ever change.'

'Well, naturally, dear, I won't if you say so.' Netta smiled, still floundering. 'I hope you're going to explain.'

'I will, later,' Kate promised, straightening.

'After church. Aidan and I always go to the early service. You two are quite welcome to join us,' she invited.

Kate paused at the door. 'Not this morning, Netta, but, if everything works out the way I think it will, we'll go this evening. That's a promise,' she gave Netta a glowing smile and went out.

Of course, some of the glow dimmed with nervousness as she made her way upstairs and along to their room. Aidan was inside, a stiff-backed silhouette over by the window. He must have heard her come in but he didn't turn. Kate shut the door quietly and relaxed back against it.

'Aidan, do you love me?' she asked him in a low, husky voice.

His start was visible, and he turned abruptly, face a dark shadow against the light outside. 'What kind of question is that?'

'A simple one, I would have thought. I just wanted to make sure, because you know I love you, don't you?' she went on in the same low tone, while her heart was skittering away inside her.

Aidan raked both hands through his hair. 'Kate, this is pointless. Loving you has nothing to do with it.'

She knew a moment of relief. He did love her. Though she hadn't seriously doubted it, still it was nice to know. It made it easier to continue.

'And I don't disgust you because of what I did?'

'Nothing about you disgusts me, Kate,' he told her huskily. 'You have to believe that.'

Her heart swelled. 'I do.'

He spread his hands. 'Then what is this all about?'

Kate clasped her hands in front of her and stared down at them. 'I thought it was about the fact that you'd decided you couldn't accept a marriage that might never be complete. That might never include children,' she said levelly.

'And I told you days ago that that wasn't so,' Aidan shot back swiftly.

Kate looked up with a smile, wondering if he realised that he was shooting down in flames all the obvious excuses he could have claimed. 'I know you did. I said I *thought* it, but then I changed my mind.'

Aidan took an audible breath, hands going to his hips. 'Kate, there had better be some point to this. I'm not made of stone!'

Pushing away from the door, she walked over to him, stopping inches away to raise her hand to his cheek, fingers gently caressing. He flinched, and she heard his swift intake of breath as he closed his eyes.

'I know you're not, Aidan, and I also know you're not Andrew,' she said softly.

His eyes shot open and locked with hers. 'Kate.' Her name was a groan.

She swallowed a lump of emotion. 'Darling, when I look at you, I see you, only you. You don't remind me of Andrew, because you're *not* him.' She had to make him believe that, as she did.

'Because I have the scar,' he agreed tautly, moving away so that her hand dropped to his chest.

Kate shook her head in vigorous denial. 'Without the scar, it would be the same. Don't you understand? My heart knows you. Every part of me responds to you as it never did to Andrew. You're two different people, and looking at you reminds me only of you. Please believe me,' she pleaded in a passionate whisper.

His handsome face broke into lines of anguish. 'I want to, and yet how can I? Kate, every time I made love to you, *he* stopped us. Last night I knew that if I slept with you, I'd make love to you, because, God knows, I want you so desperately. But I also knew it was impossible because you'd already told me you didn't know if you could forget, and in bed I only remind you of what Andrew did. I love you too much to put you through that ever again.'

Tears welled to mist her eyes. 'Aidan, listen. I didn't enjoy what happened with Andrew. I felt degraded, yes, but it's never been like that with you. You make me feel so much joy. I wanted so much to experience everything with you that I was just as shocked as you when I couldn't go on. I couldn't understand it. But now I know. *I* stopped us, not him. My own self-disgust that I could do what I did stopped me because I didn't want to remember it, and, if I'd gone on, then I believe I would have remembered sooner. But I know everything now,

and I'll learn to accept it, so that reason for backing out
has gone. I truly believe it won't happen again.'

'But you don't know for sure,' Aidan pointed out
roughly.

Kate licked her lips, because she wasn't one hundred
per cent sure. She dreaded being proved wrong, because
she knew he'd use that to enforce his decision. And yet...
'There's only one way to find out. Surely we owe it to
ourselves to give it one last try? I don't want to give you
up, Aidan, not now I've found you. Please, darling.'

'Ah, Kate! God knows I want you enough,' Aidan
groaned, reaching out to pull her into his arms. 'I just
don't want to see you hurt any more. There's been
enough pain in your life.'

'And in yours,' she insisted. 'The only thing Andrew's
done right is to bring us together. That has to mean
something.' She looked up at him, eyes pleading silently
for him to take one last chance.

His hand cupped her cheek and he sighed. 'How can
I fight you and myself? I need you as I've never needed
anyone before. You've given my life purpose. I don't
want to lose you, either. Giving you up was the hardest
decision I'd ever made. I couldn't go through that again.'

Kate's smile hid her own doubts. 'You won't have to.
Trust me. Make love with me.' Her plea was husky with
emotion.

For a moment longer he hesitated, then, with a groan
of defeat, he lifted her into his arms and carried her to
the bed. Gently he laid her down then knelt beside her,
hands smoothing her hair into a halo on the pillow about
her head. Slowly, with infinite care, he removed her
clothes until she lay before him, her creamy skin flushed
by the warmth of his gaze. She felt no fear, only an
intense pleasure as his eyes told her he found her
beautiful.

He stood up to shrug out of his own clothes, and then he came down beside her, one hand reaching out to caress her pinkened cheek. It was trembling slightly, and Kate turned her head to press a kiss to his palm, before looking at him with eyes that reflected her love and need.

Aidan swallowed. 'If anything frightens you, tell me,' he commanded thickly, head lowering to her throat, finding the pulse that beat rapidly there.

'Love me,' she murmured huskily in reply, and with a soft moan he brought his mouth up to hers.

It was like before and yet unlike anything she had ever known. With infinite patience, that drew her inexorably towards the very brink of fulfilment, his lips and hands caressed every inch of her willing, responsive flesh. Drugged by his exquisite sensuality, she couldn't think, could only feel. When his fingertips brushed across the sensitised peaks of her breasts, she moaned, arching in to him, and when he took her into his mouth, she thought she would die of the pleasure.

She had no thought of turning back, not even when his marvellous hands smoothed over her hips and traced a breathtaking path up the soft skin of her inner thigh, seeking the heart of her. When he touched her there, discovering how much she ached for him, she cried out, as waves of pleasure exploded through her at each gentle stroke.

Gasping, she gazed at him in wonderment as he raised his head to witness the havoc he had created. 'I didn't know it could feel like that,' she whispered.

Aidan smiled though his eyes smouldered with a barely leashed passion. 'That's only the beginning,' he told her thickly.

He was right, she discovered, as he began to arouse her again with a feverish passion. Limbs entangled and skin scorched skin as they scaled new heights, discovering untold plateaux of pleasure, where each delight tumbled into the next. Until, shuddering and gasping, he eased his body over hers, taking her with him as they reached the summit and toppled headlong into a dizzying explosion of mutual satisfaction.

They must have fallen asleep, for Kate came awake minutes later with the pleasurable weight of Aidan's body on her. Almost at the same instant he stirred, lifting himself up on his elbows to look at her with a warmth that melted her bones and made her heart turn over.

A slow smile spread over her face, lighting it up. 'It's just as well I'm not the sort to say I told you so,' she murmured, and caught her breath as he moved suddenly, rolling over to take her with him so that she rested comfortably on his chest.

'You can if you want. You were right, thank God. Incredibly and wonderfully right.' He sighed, catching her hand and raising it to his lips.

Kate snuggled closer, loving the warmth of him. Happiness and contentment were a cocoon about them. She sighed. 'What will happen to Andrew now?' The mention of his name had no power to destroy their happiness now, and the question had to be raised.

Beside her, Aidan tensed as scarce forgotten anger returned. 'He won't get away with it, Kate, that you can be sure of. I spoke to Dad earlier. He's going to be pulling some fairly hefty strings. I'm afraid Andrew isn't going to find life such a sinecure any more. My brother has debts. If he wants them paid he's going to have to toe the line. He's going to have to work for his money, and damned hard too. Dad's sending him to Africa. We have mining concerns out there. I think he'll be too damn busy for a long time to cause anyone any trouble.'

There was grim satisfaction in his voice, and Kate couldn't blame him. He had been hurt enough—they both had. Now was the time for healing. Her hair brushed his chin as she pressed a tender kiss to his warm flesh. She felt his immediate response as he gave a deep sigh.

'Have you any idea how much I love you, Kate Crawford? My sweet Katrine?'

Her name on his lips was a loving caress. 'Mm-hmm. Almost as much as I love you,' she declared provocatively.

'Oh, no, you've got that the wrong way round,' Aidan argued.

Kate raised her head, eyes agleam. 'I beg to differ.'

There was a light in his eyes to match hers. 'You're being argumentative, Kate. In fact, you could be called shrewish. So I only have one thing to say to that.'

Kate groaned, and freeing her hand clamped it over his mouth. 'No, you don't! Don't you dare say it! I've heard it all my adult life.'

He pulled her hand away easily. 'But never from me,' he reminded her gently, his own hand cupping her cheeks and easing her up to meet him. 'This will be different. Trust me.'

With deep reluctance, she nodded and he smiled, running his thumb tantalisingly over her lips, leaving them tingling.

His voice when he spoke was barely a whisper. 'Kiss me, Kate,' he said, and Kate smiled and did so willingly because he was right, it was different. She could have sworn he said 'I love you'.

HARLEQUIN
PROUDLY PRESENTS
A DAZZLING NEW CONCEPT IN ROMANCE FICTION

One small town—twelve terrific love stories

Welcome to Tyler, Wisconsin—a town full of people
you'll enjoy getting to know, memorable friends and
unforgettable lovers, and a long-buried secret that
lurks beneath its serene surface....

JOIN US FOR A YEAR IN THE LIFE OF TYLER

Each book set in Tyler is a self-contained love story;
together, the twelve novels stitch the fabric of a
community.

LOSE YOUR HEART TO TYLER!

The excitement begins in March 1992, with
WHIRLWIND, by Nancy Martin. When lively, brash
Liza Baron arrives home unexpectedly, she moves
into the old family lodge, where the silent and
mysterious Cliff Forrester has been living in seclusion
for years....

WATCH FOR ALL TWELVE BOOKS
OF THE TYLER SERIES
Available wherever Harlequin books are sold

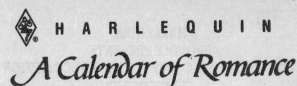

Janet Dailey
Americana

A romantic tour of America through fifty favorite Harlequin Presents novels, each one set in a different state, and researched by Janet and her husband, Bill. A journey of a lifetime in one cherished collection.

Don't miss the romantic stories set in these states:

Available wherever Harlequin books are sold.

JD-MAR

HARLEQUIN *Temptation*

Rebels & Rogues

All men are not created equal. Some are rough around the edges. Tough-minded but tenderhearted. Incredibly sexy. The tempting fulfillment of every woman's fantasy.

When it's time to fight for what they believe in, to win that special woman, our Rebels and Rogues are heroes at heart.

Matt: A hard man to forget . . . and an even harder man not to love.

THE HOOD by *Carin Rafferty.*
Temptation #381, February 1992.

Cameron: He came on a mission from light-years away. . . then a flesh-and-blood female changed everything.

THE OUTSIDER by *Barbara Delinsky.*
Temptation #385, March 1992.

At Temptation, 1992 is the Year of Rebels and Rogues. Look for twelve exciting stories, one each month, about bold and courageous men.

Don't miss upcoming books by your favorite authors, including Candace Schuler, JoAnn Ross and Janice Kaiser.

RR-2